PLAY THE GAME

C. S. SILVERNE
TILLY RIDGE

Editing: Hannah G. Wentz at English Proper Editing Services
(@englishpropereditingservices)
Cover Design & Interior Formatting: Disturbed Valkyrie Designs
(@disturbedvalkyriedesigns)

BLURB

Taking candids turned into so much more...

Marriage never looked easy on the outside looking in, but with Simon, life had been better than ever. I found my soulmate in a man who cared for me, loved me feverishly, and protected me against all odds. But regardless of the love we shared for each other, our eyes often roamed to others. Even at night, when we spent time in each other's arms, we mused over the ideas of what it would be like to explore happily again, while remaining committed to each other.

But fear always held us back.

Then *they* entered the picture.

Nyx. Asher. And Rhodes.

Our best friends.

One daring video to my husband later, and I found myself at the mercy of all four of them days later. All under the disguise of their cosplays' personas—the outfits and attitudes that started it all in the first place. Taking candids turned into so much more...

What if we can't go back to just friends?

Even if it was just supposed to be one night of fun.

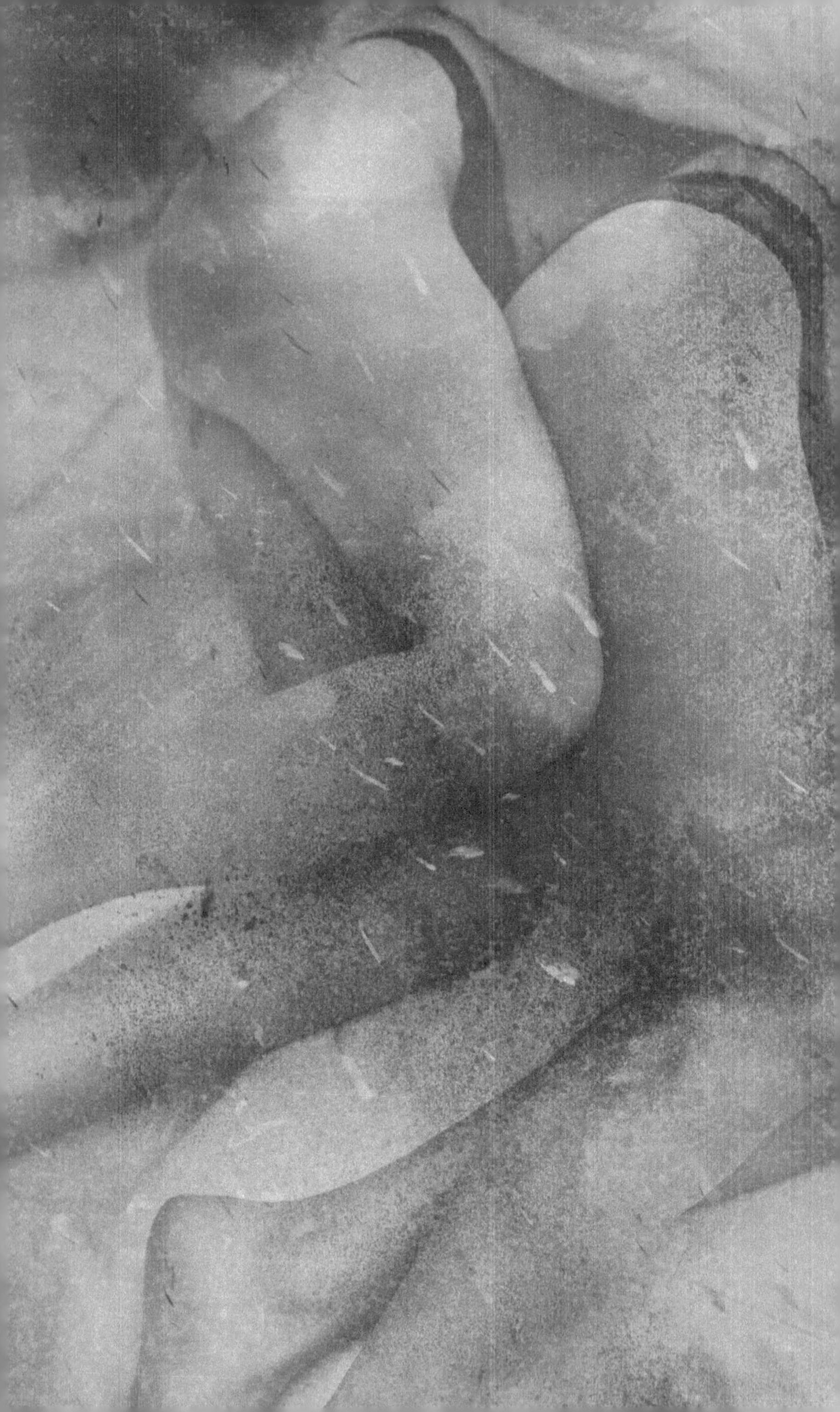

CONTENT
WARNING

Play the Game contains sensitive content. *Please protect yourself and your mental health.*

Playing recording of sexual content in front of unconsenting friends, age gap, sexual awakenings, opening a marriage, coming in pants, use of alcohol, knife play, blood play, scarification, dubious consent, degradation, praise, breeding kink, FMC speaks of being infertile (not happy or sad about it), no condom usage, spitting on genitalia, cum clean up, breath play, brat kinks, daddy/mommy/little girl play (without age play), surprise pregnancy (in epilogue), mentions of previous miscarriage (details of miscarriage are not on page), PCOS symptoms, spanking, use of toys, lesbian being called Daddy, and pegging.

PLAYLIST

Out the Roof — Chase Atlantic

Lonely Star — The Weekend

Starphucker — Beauty School Dropout (feat. Royal &
the Serpent)

self sabotage — Maggie Lindemann

She Things of Me — Landon Tewers

Devil's Playground — The Rigs

Promises — EMO

Comin' in Hot — Hollywood Undead

she knows it — Maggie Lindemann

Pull the Plug — VOILA

Rain — Sleep Token

Cravin' — Stileto & Kendyle Paige

FU In My Head — Cloudy June

Taste of the Divine — Shaker, Azee, & COBRA
Fire Up the Night — New Medicine
Incomplete — 408 & Rivals
Feel Me Now — If Not for Me
Alright — Hollywood Undead
Decode — Paramore
Hold Me Down — Halsey
If It Means A Lot To You — A Day to Remember
Paint it Black — Andy Black
DARKSIDE — Neoni
TEETH — WesGhost (feat. Diggy Graves)
Granite — Sleep Token
Go Fuck Yourself — Two Feet

LISTEN TO THE FULL PLAYLIST HERE:

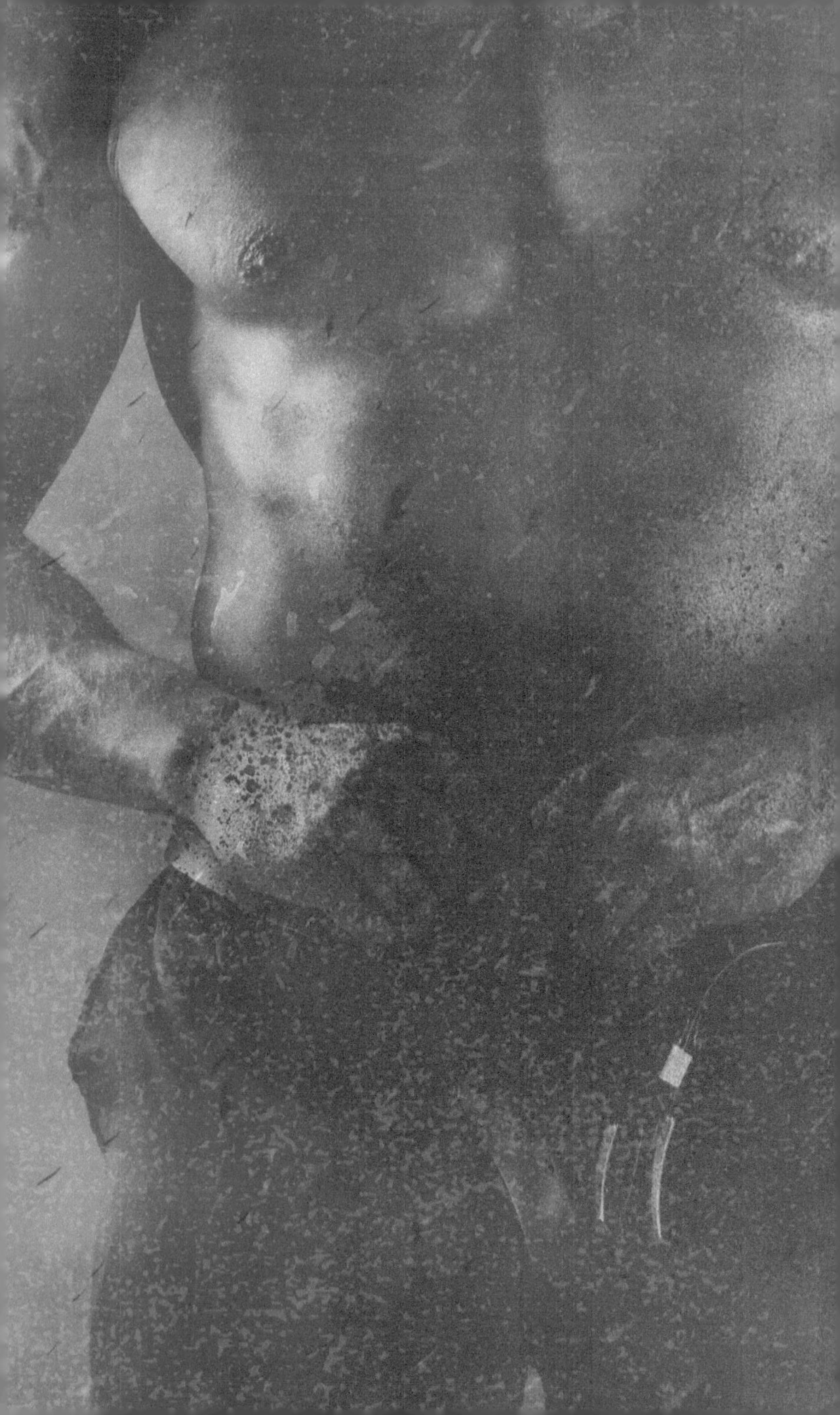

To all the Call of Duty masked tiktokers that **_don't_** threaten the bookish community, and to all of the readers who wish they would threaten them in the bedroom and **the bedroom _alone_**.

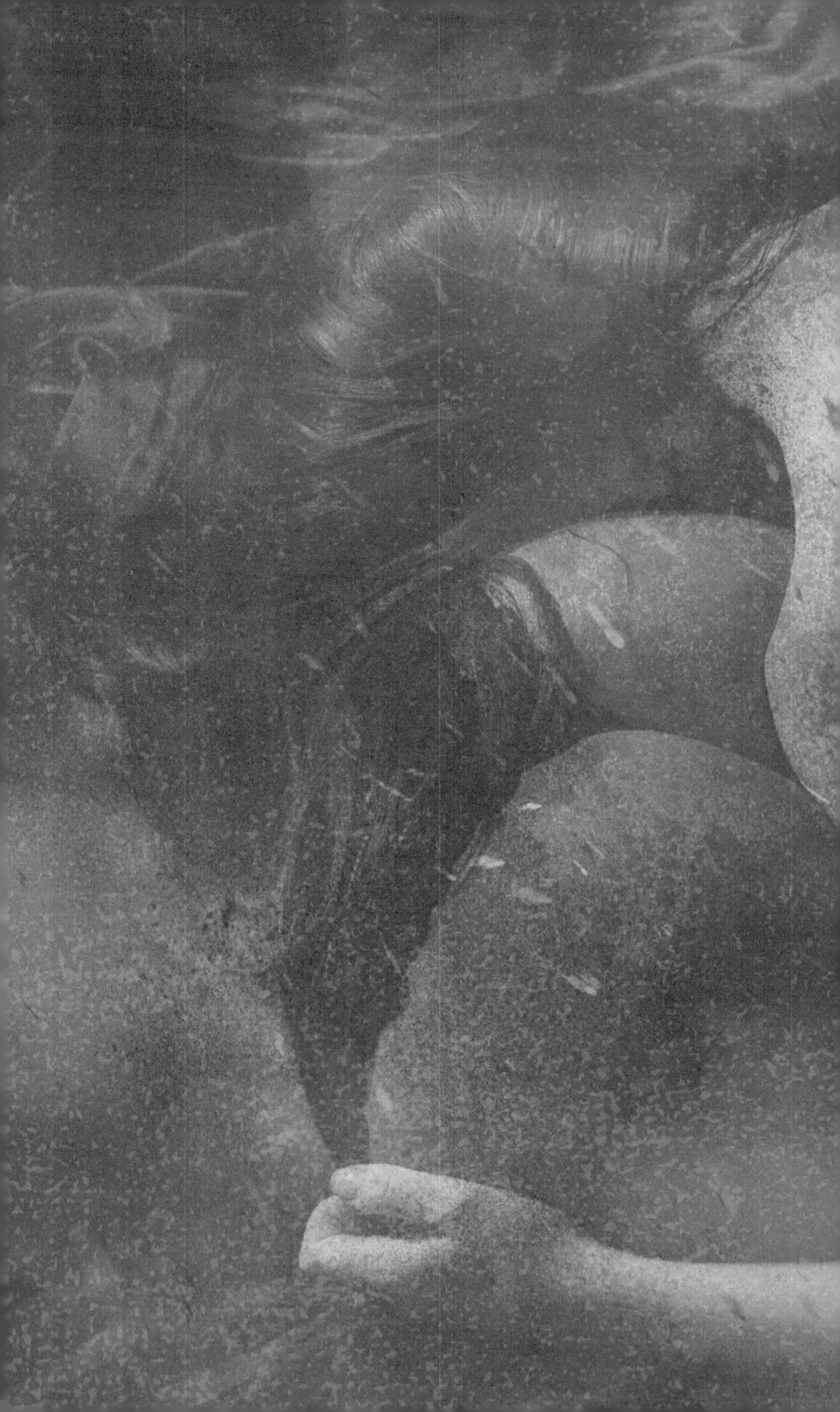

So… masked fiends—
You guys remember how the United States banned
TikTok for a whole twelve hours, and so many of our
favorite masked performers showed their true
identities… as women?

Well, Nyx says hello ;)

1

SLOANE

"You have got to be fucking kidding me," I hiss out at the dashboard, nearly seething as I wait for my husband's response through the Bluetooth speaker. Snow flurries flit around the windshield endlessly as yet another storm begins to brew towards our colder mountains, forcing me to grip the steering wheel even tighter than I already was due to my agitation at my dearest *hubby*.

Get married, they said. *It'll be fun*, they said.

I sigh at the thought petulantly.

Okay, it has its plentiful perks, and I love him with everything I have in me. This man is somehow, equivocally, everything to me. We match each other in ways that some people only think about—all the way from our love of gaming and sports, to our metal music, to the emo tattoos and clothes we always sported.

Hell, even our wedding rings are identical.

He's my best friend.

But, my best friend is currently and profoundly pissing me the fuck off.

"Babe…" Simon's deeper, smoky voice drawls. I glare down at the console once again, knowing the puppy dog pleading gaze plastered on his face, even if I can't see him. "Please? The photographer that was supposed to take our candids bailed for the night, and we're already in our full gear."

I huff obnoxiously as my hands grip the steering wheel tighter. I was going to break it if I kept at the wringing war I currently find myself in. But after the day I've had, I'm ready to choke something.

Better the steering wheel than another human, I guess.

"Simon, I am muddy, sweaty, disgusting, and even a bit wet. I cannot be seen in public like this. Can't you get someone with a smartphone to take your photos instead? It's probably just as good as anything I could do."

I know that's a lie, but fingers crossed it pacifies him.

"Wet, you say?" he asks, ignoring my point entirely.

I glare at my dashboard again, knowing the man who gave me his last name is smirking uncontrollably.

"Are you fucking kidding me right now? You beg me to help you, and then you go pervert mode, too? I am going to murder you in cold blood."

He sombers slightly, though I know the lilt in his voice from our years of dating all the same. "I'm sorry you had a bad day, baby girl. You can tell me all about it later, and I'll give you the best back rub of the century. You have my word."

I pause.

Okay, that…sounds promising.

I sniff. "With the heating oil?"

"Yes, baby."

"And your tongue fixing my attitude towards the end?"

I can hear the smile in his voice as he responds. "Yes, baby."

My hands relax against the steering wheel slightly as I breathe in deeply.

I could help him. It truly wouldn't take me long at all to shoot, edit, and manipulate only four good candids —even more so knowing they would all be hiding most of their features. All of my bitchiness is well and truly just from having a bad day, where my bride-to-be begged me to get close to a waterfall for her *fourth* set of engagement pictures, only for me to fall in, due to the weird angle.

I felt like Fiona from *Shrek*, dragging my ass out of the water, smelling like a swamp.

At least my camera, somehow, didn't take the damage.

Just my ego. And my good mood.

Simon speaks again, snapping me out of my haze. "Do I have a deal with my beautiful princess?"

"I don't know. Am I on speakerphone?" I ask. Simon has the habit of sharing his screen and personal conversations just a little too much, and I was curious if all of his best friends could hear my bitching…and the plans for future tonguing. That would be the icing on top of the cake.

The man is a green flag with his open-phone policy, and yet a red flag for the exact same reason. *Is that what kids are now calling a beige flag?*

"Yup."

"I am going to kill you, for real."

"Baby…" the word rolls out of his mouth smoothly, "you love me too much for that."

My eyes roll. He's lucky for being correct. Though, since I now know I am on speakerphone for the enjoyment of his best friends, I have a vendetta to get him to blush bright red. "Oh, just you wait, pretty boy. You're gonna be calling me Mommy very soon with that quip."

This time, it's another man's voice on the phone, who sounds distinctly like Asher. His voice is nearly as deep as Simon's, but it has a different lilt, likely due to his younger age.

The poor baby has yet to truly drop his balls.

"C'mon, Sloane. Please? I even put on my fancy ski-mask."

"Asher," I growl, seeing his bright blue, puppy dog eyes in my head. They pair too nicely with his sweet, deep, yet innocent voice, and I do *not* need his pleads added to the conversation.

"I'll beg for you," he offers, a teasing tone added to his voice. "You can call me a good boy inste—"

"Alright, alright, shut up," Simon intervenes, right as my face grows extremely hot from Asher's suggestion. Or...*flirting*. "Please, baby? You're the only one I trust, anyway. You do good work."

I sigh deeply, my resolve tumbling.

The cons of marrying your best friend?

He knows how to make you all warm, gushy, and full of butterflies.

I should've let my butterflies stay rotting and decaying like they were as a traumatized teenager.

"Fine," I grunt, flipping my turn signal as I check my mirrors to merge to the right. My exit is coming up, and even with being in the middle-of-nowhere-Colorado, it would be my luck to get a terrified driver in the snowstorm who refuses to let me merge over for my exit.

"Yes!" I hear a collective whisper-shout from all four people who have apparently been hearing more than my preferred allowance. All of Simon's best friends, who somehow also happened to live in our apartment complex, have slowly grown on me, as well.

Because who needs personal space?

I'm surprised none of them have walked in on Simon and I fucking. Or if they have, then I'm glad I don't know about it.

With annoyance laced in my voice, I speak again. "I'll be there in twenty minutes. Simon, make sure everyone is ready and in full gear, or they can suck my left tit." I then address the group of friends, lovingly annoyed. "Nyx, Asher, and Rhodes…that's not an invitation. Be fucking ready."

Asher's sweet voice comes through again. "Oh, c'mon! But I could leave the prettiest marks. I told you that I could be the goodest boy fo—"

Simon interrupts Asher again, just as my lips begin to tilt upward. "Alright, baby, I'm going to kill him. I'll see you soon."

The disconnected phone call sounds through the speakers…just as a car honks at me for going the speed limit…in a snowstorm.

It's going to be a miracle if I don't get through the rest of the day without doing something utterly and profoundly stupid.

Even as my thighs shift uncomfortably closer from the odd feelings blooming in the back of my skull at Asher's begging, Simon's possessiveness, and Nyx's and Rhodes' soft, goading laughs.

2
SLOANE

"I love you, I love you, I love you," Simon chants in my ear as his muscular, tattooed arms wrap around me. I slump forward in his arms tiredly, letting him take the brunt of my weight.

I decided to come straight to the cosplay venue rather than home and shower, because I knew that I wouldn't make it back here once I sat down on my bed.

My husband is one lucky son of a bitch.

I groan into his chest as his hug intensifies. "You better. I'm tired."

He chuckles. "I know, baby. But really," he pulls back to look into my eyes, our hazel and green gazes colliding in a sea of love and tired dominance, "thank you. You're saving our asses."

I grunt softly as I shove him away. "This is quite the set-up, ya know. You didn't tell me I'd be walking into a gamer-girl's walking, wet fantasy." And truly, it's a vision to witness. The amount of tattooed, unbelievably hot men and women around me—made even hotter by their mostly anonymous personas—is enough to send entire clans of e-girls and gamers into a frenzy.

"Oh, c'mon. You should've known from my headset alone. *Call of Duty* fiends are a completely different breed."

I snort, bending down to pick up my camera bag that I threw haphazardly at our feet in my need for a hug. "No kidding. I may know absolutely nothing about the game, but I think I'm going to have to use you a bit with this mask of yours. It's way too hot."

"Oh? We can make that happen."

And, like clockwork, Asher's voice sounds behind me. "What about me, Mommy? I thought I was gonna be the best boy ever for you."

Simon barks out before I can respond myself. "Do I need to throw you on your ass again? Stop flirting with *my wife*."

I pat his arm gently, smirking as I turn to Asher. He's in his full gear, just like Simon, though his mask is a ski mask with elaborate stitching and skull marks; very simple compared to Simon's genuinely authentic skull and night-vision headpiece. Though, as Simon's eyes are easily hidden due to their darker, earthy tones in the heavy gear, Asher's bright blue eyes stand out starkly against the black material and face paint beneath, differentiating them even more.

"Oh sweet, baby boy," I say, exaggerating my tone into a faux mock. "At least you did good and listened to Mommy by being in your full gear, hmm? Maybe I should reward the puppy after all, huh, Simon?" I ask, turning back to my husband with a smile as Asher lets out a genuine whimper from beneath his mask.

Simon points at me accusingly, though looks unfazed by my words. Although, I can't truly tell, given his entire face is covered by the shape of a Ghost skull. "You're terrible. He'll be jacking off to those words for the next year."

"I know. Now, where are the other two? Let's get this shit going."

Asher pouts behind me. "That was just unfair."

I turn to him again. "Did I say you could speak, pup?"

"No, ma'am."

"Then shut up," I reply sweetly, "and get in position so I can make you look hot."

Like an eager little kid, Simon perks up even more, forgetting about the odd interaction currently happening between Asher and myself.

"I'm already hot. Me first," he says eagerly.

My eyes roll.

Men.

However, it's Nyx's voice spoken right into my ear that makes me jump and clutch my heart through the black, puffy vest over my equally dark thermal. I didn't even know she was close to me. "I may not like men, but I'll turn them all into good puppies with you together."

I shake my head as I turn towards her, only to find Rhodes directly next to her, laughing quietly. His large, muscular shoulders that are nearly too big for his frame shake obnoxiously from the force of his laughter, though all sound is hidden beneath his dark, sheet-like mask and helmet.

That, and he's always just…too quiet. Too damaged.

Because his ex-wife robbed him of his voice enough. The absolute cunt.

The helmet and König cosplay fit him far more than he probably even knows.

Nyx speaks again, and my eyes move back to her towering over me. At my 5 '3 frame, compared to her five-foot-ten, I often feel like an infant. Not to mention, she, too, has a variation of a mask on in a balaclava style that only adds to the dominance she exhibits at all times of the day. "What do you say, *Mommy*? Want to put these boys in their place?"

My face flames, though I push through. "Always. It's good to see you. How's work been? We haven't seen you in a few weeks."

And believe me, I have noticed. A girl can only

handle so many guys around all the time. And yet, Nyx is somehow my only girl best friend.

She shrugs, dropping the teasing lilt in her voice. "Oh, I broke up with my girlfriend. She was a baby-bisexual who used me to figure out she may not be as into women as much as she thought, and she didn't want to settle down anytime soon. So, I sulked in my apartment and buried myself in my to-do list for a few weeks. Work has been fine."

I nod sympathetically. Being bisexual myself, I do not miss those days. I understand her pain far more than I want to. "Why do you always get the baby bis? We need to find you someone firmly and comfortably *outside* of the closet for once."

She hums, looking me up and down. "Are you volunteering?"

Simon wraps a protective arm around me, dragging me closer to him as I take my camera out of its protective sleeve. I snuggle my back into his warmth as I look down at it, altering the settings needed for singular portraits and indoor, biting back my smile at his response. "If one more person flirts with my *fucking* wife tonight, I'm kicking their asses."

This time, it's Rhodes who speaks, "No worries there. She smells like a lake. Did you go fishing today?"

My hidden smile drops immediately, and with a growl, I decide I am never helping my friends again.

Even if they're way too fucking hot in their flirting tones and set-ups.

ME

That shower was heavenly.

SIMON

That's wonderful baby. I'm glad you feel better.

ME

So much better. I think I can be a nice human now.

SIMON

Lovely. Make sure to go eat something, too.

ME

But I need to edit your stupid pictures, remember? Someone needs them by this weekend?

SIMON

And you can do that (please)...after you eat a sandwich.

ME

I think I need an orgasm, too.

SIMON

Oh, dear Gods. That took a turn.

ME

When will you be done tonight?
Rhodes' apartment, right?

SIMON

Mmmhhmmm. We'll be playing late
tonight. It's a competitive, ranked
night. Leading up to the weekend
event. That's what we needed the
photos for.

But I promise, I'll still give you that
massage and tonguing later.

ME

I know you will.

I'll just get myself ready for it.

SIMON

You heathen.

Asher saw that btw. He wants to know
what you meant.

ME

Enjoy your game

I SIGH AS I THREW MY PHONE ON THE COUCH AND MOVE towards the fridge, hungrier than hell. I will never admit to the man that I am following his orders of eating before I edit their photos, solely because he already knows me a little too well, but I'll be damned if I don't put food in my stomach as soon as possible.

No wonder I was a bitch earlier. I haven't eaten since ten in the morning, and it is nearing seven at night now. As I make my pitiful dinner, I truly can't help but let my mind wander to everyone's comments from just hours earlier.

Simon's possessive touches and words.

Asher's begging, pleading, and overall good-boy being self.

Nyx's flirtations.

Even Rhodes, once he was done being an asshole and commenting on my smell, had winked at me a few times under his sheet…after he had caught me staring at his veiny and muscular forearms just a little too long.

I scoff at the fact of being caught.

Once again, from the memory of them all, my thighs shift together on their own.

Needingly.

I refused to touch myself in the shower, between the exhaustion and confusion over what I'm even horny about, but I don't think I can hold out for much longer.

Especially not as a deep, longing ache begins to spread through my core. The ache to take it rougher than normal, with all of the masked men and women, and their darker personas floating through my brain.

Reaching for my laptop, I sigh as I connect my camera to my hard drive with my handy USB-C adapter, and carry the entire setup, plus the plate holding my sandwich, to the couch.

Multi-tasking.

Thank you, ADHD medication.

As I simultaneously eat and edited, the thoughts refuse to slow down.

"I'll be a good boy for you, Mommy," Asher's whimper echoes in my skull. His baby blues are staring at me from the laptop screen.

"What do you say, Mommy? Want to put these boys in their place," Nyx's statements plays in my head next.

"Do I need to throw you on your ass again? Stop flirting with my wife." Simon repeats, and my brain all but purrs.

Rhodes' catching my eye-fucking was only the cherry on the top, with his challenging stare. A stare that promised more flirting than all of the words combined.

Quickly, abandoning both my laptop and plate, I snatch up my phone from the other end of the couch and began making my way to the bedroom, right where I know our toy chest is.

I am breaking.

Shattering.

I can play by myself, to shake the needy feeling I can't escape.

But Simon has forced me not only to work late, but deal with all of his friend's flirting moods. And masked hotness.

I think he deserves a little payback while he is having his fun with our friends.

Just in a way that will make him weak in the knees. Like the good *wifey* I am.

3

SIMON

Conventions always take it out of me…but instead of going home and crashing with my wife, what am I doing? Following Rhodes and the rest of our crew into his apartment.

Luckily, we all live in the same complex, so if any of us ever get too rowdy, whoever was voted to stay moderately sober that night has to walk us home. Or we end up crashing on whoever is hosting's couch.

We're getting too old for the couch shit…my back can't handle another night of that.

Sloane went back to our place to get a head start on editing all of the photos she took of us at the convention today. I feel it was to appreciate my friends in their cosplay gear *comfortably*, away from the judgmental eyes at the convention.

Who can blame her, I openly ogle them all the time. *They're hot.*

She usually sits and reads off to the side when we're gaming as it is, but she has a slight glee in her eyes when we part ways in the parking lot that gives her away. Her being a photographer couldn't have worked out better for this little hobby I picked up randomly a year or so ago. I never thought there would be so much interest in some random man on the internet dressing up in gear from one of my favorite games, but here I am, making astronomical amounts of money from it. All while having the time of my life with my three best friends.

It's cold as fuck here in Manitou Springs, tucked up in the mountains of Colorado. The end of January is some of the coldest weeks; tonight is nothing shy of that. As Rhodes pushes his door open, I'm on the verge of cheering when the heat hits my body as we walk into his apartment.

His cat comes straight towards me, weaving in and out of my legs. Rhodes goes straight to the kitchen to put out Rouge's wet food. Seeing that big man melt for that cat is something I never thought I would witness, but he rescued Rouge when he was a kitten last winter. And now that black cat runs this apartment like it's his.

No one is complaining…he's the cutest little thing.

While Rhodes is in the kitchen, Asher, Nyx, and I start setting up the living room to game. I flop down in the middle of the couch, and the two of them take a seat on either side of me. Rhodes has his massive gaming chair, which he always claims.

We start up the four-player mode of *Call of Duty: Black Ops*, and we all settle in for some fun. Our beers are cold and the shit-talking is ready to go.

Before any of us know it, it's been at least an hour or two of playing. My phone lights up on the coffee table in front of us.

I see Sloane's name pop up on the screen.

SLOANE

The masks do it for me...

Incoming 😊

video attached

Oh fuck.

In a split-second decision, I hit play on the video I know was sent to just me—but at the same time, she knew I was here gaming with the group...maybe she wants them to see, too?

Maybe *I* want them to see?

No, I know I want them to see, but does my wife?

The video plays and she's all hot and bothered, pleasing herself and that gorgeous cunt between her legs, from what I can only imagine is the pictures of us that she's editing.

The cunt that's been all mine for the past three years.

We talk about opening our marriage often, but never end up going through with it. Not because either of us is unhappy with one another, but because both of us are bisexual. It only makes sense to be able to explore and eventually add to our perfect marriage. Why keep all the love we have to offer to just us? It just hasn't been the right time…

But today looks to be the day.

I crank the volume up on my phone, hoping it gets the attention of my friends.

Friends who are all single at this point.

Nyx is the freshest out of a relationship. It's been three months since she finally broke up with her most recent girlfriend, and fuck, was it a nasty breakup. We've all been taking turns ensuring she's good, and she has been, thankfully. I think she realized quickly, once out of the relationship, how beyond toxic they were together.

I've never seen Asher with a partner. I have seen a booty call coming or going, but nothing serious for him. He's so young, I would've been worried if he *had* previously been in a super-long relationship.

And Rhodes…

I haven't seen him with anyone since he left his wife of ten years a couple of years back. She cheated on him over and over for pretty much their whole marriage, and I think that broke him deeper than anything I could ever imagine. We talk about it here and there, of why he thought he needed to stay and work through it all. He was raised extremely religious, and it was ingrained in him that divorce was never an option, but he eventually left. We all joked with one another that he's just the old, lonely cat man, but I've stopped because I see those comments hit him way too deep.

It makes my soul ache to see my friends not trust love or think they're unworthy of it. I want them to be able to have the love they all deserve.

The moan from Sloane through my phone is louder than I thought it would be. She breathlessly groans, "Fuck, you all are so hot with your masks on." All three sets of eyes turn to me, and I just give them the most devilish grin I can muster up right now. "I couldn't get through the pictures without touching myself," she shyly murmurs the last sentence. And *fuck*, is my cock paying attention.

Nyx looks over at my phone, questioning, "Is that Sloane? Simon, what the fuck are you doing playing that right now?" She might be acting pissed at me, but she sure as hell doesn't have the willpower to take her eyes off my wife's beautiful cunt. The tension between the two of them is always so thick, yet neither will ever cross the line that they both dance on together.

I question Asher and Nyx, completely ignoring her question, "Isn't she so fucking pretty like this?"

That question causes Rhodes to leave his gaming chair and lean over me to see the ruckus.

"We can walk you to your place if you need to help her…" Asher leans over to take a harder look at my phone, and I can't blame him one fucking bit. He murmurs, "Fuck, it looks like she could use some help."

Finally, I have the courage to ask the question that Sloane and I have wanted to ask them all for a while now: "Would you all want to help? Or play?" No matter what their answers are, our friendships are forever changed. There's no returning from watching someone's wife play with themselves; let alone ask them to fuck around with you and your wife, and think you can keep the same connections you had previously. But to see my wife's fantasies come to life, it would all be worth it.

And selfishly, my fantasies would be coming true, as well…

They all have given me hints that they would play if we were ever to ask them, but they never made the first move. No one answers my question. They all just look at me like I've lost my ever-loving mind.

So I go all out.

After hitting a couple of buttons on my phone, the video of my wife is now playing on the TV, the game completely forgotten.

"*Fuck.*" Rhodes wipes a hand down his face and

covers his mouth while watching my beautiful wife on the screen. He heads back to his seat, but stays slightly turned so I can still see his reactions.

I look at Asher, and his eyes haven't left the screen, either. I'm practically growling in his ear, "You like older women, don't you, Asher?" He whips his head to the side, and I see the slight panic in his eyes from being so close to my face.

I relish in it.

It's been too long since I've been this close to another man, and fuck, have I missed it. His citrus and woody scent fills my senses.

It's heady.

I move in an inch, stay there long enough to see the panic take over him, and then lay back on the couch. Scooting my ass out and spreading my legs obnoxiously wide, making sure I place a knee against Asher's, I let Sloane do the talking for us.

She has her laptop open and off to the side on our couch, and we can see her screen clear as day. It's all of us in our gear, pulled up in her editing program. She whispers, looking right into the camera, "Why are our friends so fucking hot?" Rhodes' head snaps to look at me, and I just give him a sly smile and a head nod.

Sloane's doing all the hard work for me here.

We watch in silence as she circles her clit with one hand while being propped up by the back of the couch, her other fingers getting sucked in between her pouty lips. She slowly trails those same fingers down her stomach and inserts two fingers, causing herself to moan. That moan travels to my cock like it's connected to everything that is her. Pushing her tits together between her arms, they're on full display. The heart-shaped jewelry encase those raspberry nipples I love so much.

Nyx mumbles, "I had a feeling she had her nipples pierced, but fuck, her tits are perfect." She gives me an appreciative smile.

She's close to coming.

I can feel my cock leaking behind my cargo pants, and I can see Rhodes's cock, matching mine.

"I'm so close. Fuck, I'm so clossseee."

The balled-up fists Asher is sporting has me slightly worried…he almost looks like he's in pain.

Between gasps for air, Sloane moans, "I'm coming, coming for all of you."

The TV screen goes black and we all just sit there for a moment in silence.

Asher breaks the silence, lifting his head off the back of the couch. "Well, this is embarrassing…" We all look over to where his eyes are…his crotch.

Oh shit…he came in his pants.

"That's hot as fuck," I encourage him.

Rhodes chimes in, "I was close to blowing in my pants, too. Shit, I'm surprised I didn't…that's the most action I've had in a long time."

We're all laughing, and I hate that it's at Rhodes' lack of a sex life, but it does the job of lightening the mood for a brief second.

I bring up my question from earlier, "So, do you all want to play with us?"

I'm hit with "hell yes" from Nyx, a "fuck yes" from Rhodes, and the shyest "yeah" from Asher.

Walking back to my apartment alone tonight consists of scheming one of the best football parties that'll, hopefully, turn into a full-on orgy by the end of the night.

And with all of our friends on board, I start to plan the night that I know will change our lives forever.

Then it hits me.

I'll code a power outage for right after the big performance at halftime. That's the only reason Sloane even watches.

Well, that and the commercials.

The excitement for what this can mean for us has me practically bouncing on my feet as I walk through our front door.

Here's to everything changing.

Let's hope it's for the good.

4

SLOANE

A firm, muscular, heavily tattooed arm wraps around my waist, dragging me into an equally firm and tattooed chest. My hair falls around us in a blanket of security and I sigh comfortingly in the warmth that belongs to this man.

"Good morning, beautiful."

"Nuh-uh," I whisper back as I turn my face back into the pillows. Just because I love this man does not mean that I want to talk to him yet. "Go back to sleep."

"I haven't slept yet, actually."

My head snaps up as I shoot my eyes to the alarm clock on our nightstand, right next to the small ghost-shaped dish that always holds our wedding bands. Both engraved with snakes, like the emo trash we absolutely are.

"What the fuck?" My voice comes out groggy as I turn towards him. "It's seven in the morning. Why haven't you slept?"

His eyes nearly sparkle as he responds, "I don't know. Someone sent me a very, very naughty video while I was with the group, that has been replaying in my mind for hours."

A blush immediately marks my face.

I wasn't even drinking last night. Can't blame any fantasy on the booze this time.

"And?" I ask, trying to appear braver than I feel.

"And…" Simon responds, shifting us so that we're no longer spooning. Instead, I'm on my back as he towers over me, placing his weight on his hands, right beside my head. The man spends hours in the gym, almost daily, and it always strikes me as intense whenever he can do fucking *planks* above me without even flinching. "I enjoyed it very much."

I smile. "Yeah? Even with the other guys on the screen? You seemed so big and bad at the convention, so I didn't know how we were feeling there."

"Pffft," he scoffs, "c'mon, baby girl. I think you know how hard my dick actually gets to the thought of other men or women touching you. But that's for us, until we make a plan for otherwise."

I nod, even as my stomach sinks slightly at his words.

That's the issue. All talk, no action.

Though, I had long-since relayed to myself that this would always be an interesting discussion within the boundaries of our marriage. Opening a marriage was… unbelievably daunting.

Having fantasies about fucking your husband's best friends was much easier than actually doing it.

"Right. Yeah," I nod and smile up at him, "just for us."

He sees right through it. *The absolute bastard.* "Unless, you were ready to take that step?"

"I'm good where I am if you are."

"And if I'm not?"

Now, I sigh. It's fueled with a mixture of agitation, annoyance, and bratty snark. I am damn tired of always having a say regarding this topic. "Then make the first move so I can figure out my life, Simon."

All of a sudden, his weight shifts to a singular hand, though he balances himself as he drags a knee down in between my legs. I gasp at the sudden pressure, though I find myself silenced as his hand covers my mouth. His rough voice grows heavier. "Do I sense an attitude still in you, pretty girl? I thought we were just talking."

I lick his hand over my mouth, but he doesn't even flinch.

We were just talking.

But I'm a scared girl, at the end of the day, who will never risk losing my best friend on my own accord. And I don't know how else to get it through his skull that I'm ready for a change.

Just as long as I don't have to be the one who pulls the trigger.

"Mmmm," he growls out. "I would normally get your paddle out for such an attitude over the last few days, but I think you just need some loving today. Don't you?"

My eyes roll.

In pleasure, from the pressure of his knee digging in even more, or from annoyance over more softness, I can't tell.

But I also wouldn't fight a good oral session, either.

This man knows how to pleasure a woman, and I am always okay with it.

Finally, he releases his hand from my mouth and leans down to kiss me hungrily. Hungry enough for me to think, *we'll be just fine.*

Because that's a kiss that held more of a promise than anything he's said or done yet.

Even as he climbs down my body to *finally* fix my attitude.

And I welcome him happily, because we have a party to prepare for, and I will have to look all of our best friends in the eyes, knowing it was actually them I was fingering myself to the night before, rather than my just beautiful husband.

5
SLOANE

"Babe!" Simon's voice echoes throughout the small apartment, tone deafening so I can hear him over the music, conveniently seconds after the absolute pounding our door just took. Between his shout, the envy over the poor *door*, and the liquor burning at my throat, I choke lightly, forcing my eyes to water against the freshly applied mascara. "Are you decent? They're here!"

I poke my head out of the bathroom, coughing lightly. "I mean, I'm in a t-shirt and booty shorts? I think they'll be fine. They've probably seen me in worse condition."

Instantly, his face turns bright red.

Dread sinks in my stomach as I stare at him. "What?

Oh my God, I knew it! They have caught us having sex, haven't they?"

With a firm hand, he hits his left peck, almost like he's forcing his heart to restart beating with the singular, Oscar-worthy hit. His response is quick and hurried as he shyly turns away from me, avoiding eye contact. "Yeah. Yeah, a few months ago. They didn't want to embarrass you, though."

I groan as I turn back towards the bathroom, still needing to do my makeup. I was too busy cooking appetizers for the amount of testosterone that was about to grace our humble abode that I hardly realized it was later than preferred by the time I started getting ready.

Turns out, instead of just correcting my attitude this morning, Simon actually had hours of edging and begging in store for me.

I hate him, just as much as I adore him.

"What do they care if they see my ass cheeks, then?" I shout against the deafening tones of Hollywood Undead's *Comin in Hot.* "Maybe they'll like it, knowing I'm a moaner now. Just let them in."

I could have sworn I heard the distinct sound of my husband's snort, even over the music.

He's lucky that he's so pretty.

Leaning over the bathroom sink, I sing the lyrics with a little dance as I wipe away at the residue from my choking fit, only to reapply the mascara once again. The strength of the tequila is coating my entire body in a sense of comforting, buzzing warmth, and it would be a damn shame to not dance it out.

"Well, if this isn't a lovely sight, I don't know what is," I hear to my right, forcing me to look away from my blush-coated reflection and directly into the humorous gaze of Rhodes.

I smile at him, right as his eyes go down and nearly lock on my boobs. Right where my nipples are pointed, outlined by the piercings they carry. "Happy football Sunday to you, too, silly goose."

He swallows roughly before moving back to my face. His eyes are hard, and it nearly feels analytical. "Happy day, beautiful. Are you ready for the night of your life?"

I snort and turn back towards the mirror once again, feeling my own ass bounce lightly from the movement. I can only hope that the tattoo that says *good girl* in a dainty script, right below my ass cheek, catches his attention. "Oh yeah," I say sarcastically, "I can't wait to watch teams I don't care about while you and the mongrels eat all my food. Why did I agree to hosting this year?"

Before I know it, he's straying from his typical eye roll response, and instead I find myself staring at his bulky reflection as he walks into the bathroom with me.

The small, tight bathroom.

Small enough that we're forced to stand with his front pressed against my back. I gasp lightly as I swear I feel the shape of a bulge pressing into the indent of my back.

"Are you always such a smartass?"

I swallow roughly as I match his intense gaze in the mirror. This feels innately intimate. More intimate than my possessive husband would ever be comfortable with. "You know the answer to that."

He laughs darkly as he bends down. The motion forces me to shiver against him. He keeps eye contact with me, even as he brushes the barest kiss against my t-shirt-covered shoulder. "That, I do."

It's Simon's voice that breaks the tense, lust-filled bubble surrounding us, forcing me to lean away from Rhodes and even closer to the mirror—that shows my face being the color of a firetruck. "Glad to see you two are actually getting along for once. Do you have room for one more?"

My eyes snap to him, alarmed.

He's not angry.

He's not…turning into a caveman.

What the fuck?

Rhodes speaks for me, our eyes landing on one another once more in the mirror before a sly smile takes over his face. "I think we always got along. I just didn't realize how much I was allowed to appreciate her, though."

"Appreciate her all you'd like. You were the only one who didn't flirt with her at the con, anyways."

Rhodes turns away from my blushing, panicked, lust-filled gaze, only to lock heavy eyes with Simon. With a nod, he pats his shoulder in some weird, brotherly way before he walks away in the direction of our living room. But not before he throws the most confusing sentence over his shoulder. "Yeah. The amount of changes that can happen so soon, right?"

Simon swallows before leaning into the bathroom and kissing me on the cheek. "You do look beautiful," he mutters, before following after Rhodes.

And as Hollywood Undead continues playing, I'm left thinking, once again…

What the fuck?

"C'MON, DUDE," NYX SAYS AS SHE GRABS MY KINDLE from me as I sit on the couch. "We're at your party, and you're still hiding in a corner, reading? This is only allowed at other people's houses."

I pout and give grabby hands towards my Kindle. "Hey! I was at a good part!"

"What are you even reading now? Don't you have enough physical books?"

I blush and tip my head back, groaning. I already started to feel overstimulated hours ago, courtesy of the skin-tight jeans I changed into—which drive Simon crazy—and reading was my comfort activity in said moments. Paired with the guy's shouts as we grew closer to halftime, I was antsy as fuck. And probably needing more liquor. "Just some new, smutty, romance. It doesn't matter. Gimmie!"

"Or what, little heathen? Are you going to pout and beg for it back? I'd like to be called Mommy, if you're going to."

All at once, my brain clouded in a mountain of dazed lust as I stared up at her.

For fuck's sake.

I need them all to stop being so intense.

I push through the fog covering my brain. The fog that, coincidentally, is reminding me that it's been years since I've let another woman touch me, and damn, if I didn't miss it.

I've missed begging for a Mommy.

"I need another drink."

She smiles brightly, nodding her head, and throws my Kindle to the other side of the couch. Directly on Asher's lap, which is thankfully covered by a pillow as he stares intently at the screen. "That's my girl. Get me one too, please!"

I groan as I stand up. "Yes, Mommy," I draw out.

I stop in my tracks, right as I go to enter the kitchen. Because the fucking power cuts off, forcing us all into a bubble of dark silence.

You have got to be fucking kidding me.

"Simon!" I shout, moving back towards the living room. "What the fuck? Is it the snowstorm?"

All three of the men, and even Nyx, stare at the now blackened-out TV screen in a fit of annoyance and shock.

"Okay," I say, annoyance heavy in my tone. "No one is more pissed off than me. I really wanted to see that concert! Simon, does our apartment have a backup generator?"

He shakes his head as he turns to me, eyes heavy.

Damn.

He must have really wanted to see that last play of the night.

"No, I don't think so. I don't even think we have any flashlights."

My shoulders slump down. "Are you kidding? We have nothing but scented candles that'll make our apartment smell like a bakery?"

Nyx speaks up, excitement in her tone as she goes to stand. "You guys have a flashlight! I saw one under the sink when I had to get tampons last time I was here. I'll go get it. I have to pee, anyway."

Rhodes speaks next. "I have some at my place? Asher, you wanna check your apartment, too?"

Asher's face blushes bright red as all eyes fall on him, and he mutters shyly, "Yeah, yeah I can go check. See if I can find anything."

Simon claps, and automatically, they're all standing. I squint at every one of them. "You all have to go check for flashlights? You know this is how the main character normally gets murdered, right? Why do I have to be alone?"

"Rude!" Nyx shouts from the bathroom. "I'm right here, you drunk bitch. Let them go be boys. Maybe the murderer will get them first."

Simon chuckles and leans down to kiss my cheek. "You're fine. Everything is fine. We'll be right back, okay?"

Rhodes continues behind him, while Asher keeps his head down and walks right out the door, still blushing profusely. "No one is getting through to Simon and me, Sloane. Chill out. We'll feed them Asher if they do," Rhodes offers.

And somehow, seconds later, I find myself standing alone in my dark and quickly cooling apartment.

My anxiety turns on its head as I make my way back into the kitchen.

Now I really need that drink.

6

SIMON

"Let's run through the plan one more time…" Poor Asher is so stressed from what's about to go down, but I've given him every chance to back out and he wants to have a role in this game that we're about to play.

A game that involves my marriage.

My friendships.

All the people I care about so deeply are being brought together in the best way I could imagine. The two people with me, including Nyx, who's in our spare bathroom changing as we speak, are the most kind-hearted people I've had the pleasure of meeting, and we get to bring them into what we have as a husband and wife. Even if it is only for tonight, and we're right back to best of buds after.

I don't think that will be the case, but you never know…Is it bad that I'm already planning a future for the five of us, and I have no clue where any of their heads are?

Including my wife…

Yeah, that's bad.

The words are on the tip of my tongue to finally answer Asher going over the plan for what feels like the fifteenth time just today. But the words don't form as a super jacked Rhodes pulls his raggy old t-shirt over his head with one hand.

Dear fucking God, his body will never not impress me. He's two inches shorter than my six-foot-five frame, but he's the definition of a *big boy*. Not to mention the tattoos that cover his broad chest and shoulder—the beefiest shoulder I've ever seen. He's the kind of big man who never steps in the gym, but has a body that could throw a grown man over his shoulder and get where he needs to go. The kind of muscles that are from his blue-collar job lifting and doing shit that would blow your mind.

My kryptonite look on a man.

Finally, I remember to answer Asher's question. "I rigged the code for our apartment for the electricity to go out for at least an hour. We'll get dressed in our gear, bust in the door, and ambush her from every side, including Nyx. She's in the bathroom changing. She wants to be scared. She wants the fear. It gets her soaked." The smirk on my lips is sinister, and I turn to Rhodes to see his lips match mine.

Noted.

Big man likes to cause fear.

Asher looks more scared than I think Sloane will after what I explained to him, so I add, "She wants this, Asher. I promise. Actually…I don't have to promise. You heard her on the video."

Asher blushes.

Full-on blushes, which might be my new favorite thing he can do. He's the same height as Rhodes, but their bodies couldn't be more different. Asher's a lot slimmer, but his muscles are *defined*, and his abs make me want to drag my tongue up them, to explore up close. I know his are built in the gym like mine are, because he's my gym buddy. Those arms he's built are littered with colorful, random tattoos—but my favorite thing on this body of his is the barbell through one of his nipples.

And now my cock is hard…great.

Ignoring the growing member in my pants, I slide my thin spandex material mask on my head, and get my headgear in place. In my mind, I know Sloane will know who we are just from our specific gear, but this has always been one of her fantasies, and I can't wait to watch it come to life.

Rhodes gets his mask into place, and once I can see his eyes through the only holes on his blanket-type mask, I know he's more than ready to have his way with my wife.

Honestly, maybe me, too…he looks starving.

Rhodes places his black helmet on to finish out his gear. Asher slides his balaclava skull-style mask over his beautiful face. The fact that I can still see his sickly, harsh jawline makes me want to bite my fist and then scream into the void.

Running my eyes over both of them, ensuring we're ready, I then ask both of them, "You all ready to make our fantasies come to life?"

Rhodes automatically answers me, "Hell yes!"

But when I look back at Asher, I see that he's between Rhodes and I. He mumbles, "Are you sure about this, Simon? I don't want our friendship going to shit after this."

I pull my phone out and send the group chat a text that Nyx will hopefully see.

PLAY THE GAME GC

ME

Give us three minutes, and we'll be busting the door in

NYX

10/4 bossman

"Just follow our lead, Asher. Call red if you want

anything to stop and yellow if you need to slow down, we will all listen." Now Rhodes is comforting Asher, and I think my heart is expanding by the second.

I decide to tease Asher. "Pull the *okay, Mommy* energy out that you had at the con. You'll be fine!"

And with that, we're locking up Asher's apartment for the night and heading across the pathway to my door.

With both of them at my back, knowing we have a huge door stopper on the wall, I crack the door and kick it with all my might. It slams open, and my eyes land on my beautiful wife at the end of the entry hallway. I lean my head down but keep my eyes locked with hers, hoping Rhodes and Asher are following my lead.

My scared shitless wife, might I add.

I grin, but she can't see it because my mask obscures her view. Seeing the fear line her features, shift over to recognition, then morph right back to being scared again sends my cock jumping behind my zipper.

I pull my knife out of my belt holster and start stalking towards her. I hear Asher gasp when he spots the knife in my hand. Then, out of nowhere, Nyx is busting out of the hall bathroom behind Sloane. She's charging Sloane and immediately pulling her arms behind her back, slapping cuffs onto her wrists.

Rhodes's deep timber starts. "The fuck toy has a nice rack."

She does indeed, but they've already seen her

glorious body on display. I can't wait to watch them explore her inch by inch.

The guys stop a couple of feet from Sloane and Nyx, but I start to circle them. Nyx takes the cue, whispers something into Sloane's ear that has her whimpering, and then heads over to stand with the guys.

I circle her twice, looking Sloane, my wife, up and down. When I'm back to her front, I press the tip of my knife into the zipper of her black jeans.

My favorite pair of hers that makes her ass look otherworldly.

I slowly drag the flat side of the blade up her stomach, meeting the bottom seam of her black, V-neck crop top that's just above her belly button. I hold my knife there for a second, flip it around to where the sharp side is lined up toward me, then pull.

Her tight little shirt busts open, exposing her emerald green, lace bra.

My favorite bra she owns.

She has every one of my favorites on tonight, and I'm sending a thank-you note to the devil for that.

She gasps and nervously whispers, "Please don't."

Out of my peripheral, I see Asher take a step towards us like he needs to step in…like I can't be stopped. I throw my hand up, signaling him to halt, and he does just that. I pull the skeleton fingered black gloves off of my left hand, and hold it up in front of Sloane's face.

Crossing her body, she places her left hand in mine, lining up our matching black wedding bands with one another. Letting her know it's me, like she didn't already know. She gives a slight smile to Asher and a quick head nod, reassuring him. He falls back beside Rhodes again.

Slipping my glove back on, I start to degrade her. This will have her dripping for us, as if she's not already. "Is this what my whore of a wife wanted? To be used and abused by our best friends?" But what shocks me the most is the quietest whimper creeping up Asher's throat at my words.

She whimpers at that. "Yessss please, Daddy." I place the tip of my knife right under the soft part below her chin.

Testing the waters with Asher, I look over my shoulder at him. "Mmm, do we have another whore on our hands?" I can tell he's unsure, so I dip my head again, letting him know I'm serious. "Good boys answer the first time they're asked a question."

He immediately answers, "Yes, Daddy."

Fuck.

7

SIMON

"What are you going to do to me?" Sloane's voice shakes.

Oh, she's *really* putting the show on now. The strain my cock has against my pants says everything about how much I'm eating this little show of hers up; it'll be giving me away to our friends in no time.

As I stand behind her, I place the more rigid skull part of my mask against her ear, ensuring she hears me sniffing her scent before I say, "I'm going to make my soldiers watch me fuck you until you're dripping with my cum. Then, they can use this body however they please." The gasp that comes from her is music to my ears.

"Fuckkkk," Rhodes moans, and I swear to all things holy, I'm not going to survive this. I shift my hips and, in turn, shove my cock into Sloane's back, hoping it keeps me from coming in my pants and embarrassing myself. Her tight little body shivers against my front, and the smile lining my lips under my mask would be blinding if anyone could see it.

I know this is why she was being bratty this morning—waiting for me to tell her I agreed to play with all of our friends like she was fantasizing about in the little video she sent me last night. I didn't want to ruin the surprise because seeing her reactions would only be made better if our friends got to see them as well. I also know that she's been ready for this for a while now, and I know I have been, too, now that I think back on it…it just never felt like the right time.

But now.

Today…it's the perfect time for a friends'-fuck-fest.

I pull my front away from her, spin her around to fully face our friends, and step back beside them to watch her. I give the command I've been waiting to say all night. "We won't wait much longer…" I know for a fact each one of them would wait years to see my beautiful wife strip in front of them, but Sloane doesn't need to know that. "Strip. Nice and slow. Let them see how needy that body is for me. For *us*."

I see the glint in her eyes. She wants to brat, but hasn't yet. To say I'm ready to dull this punishment out is an understatement. She slowly reaches for the button on her jeans, pops it open, and lets the zipper fall to the bottom. Pulling them down her gorgeous thighs and to her feet, she tosses them off into the kitchen.

Thankfully, Sloane found all the candles and has lit them throughout the apartment. She was right: it smells like a goddamn bakery in here. But it's giving us enough light, and I won't lie and say it's not helping set the vibes with the moody lighting.

She's in her lacey, matching emerald green thong. The matching set she knows I'm obsessed with. I got it for her when I stumbled across it in a lingerie ad. Seeing her heart-shaped nipple rings hitting the light through the dark lace that's covering her perfect tits, makes my body vibrate with need.

On a hum, I tell her, "Spin for us, baby. Show our friends that lovely body of yours in my favorite lingerie." And she does just that.

Spinning on her heels, Nyx is quick with her words. "I've waited to see your wife like this for way too long, Simon. You're one lucky bastard."

"I am, aren't I?" Nyx just nods, agreeing with me while too lost in my wife.

I step back up to her and pull her chin up with my thumb and pointer finger, lifting my mask up enough to free my lips. Pressing mine to hers I pull back enough to murmur, "You call red and everything stops, baby."

"Condoms?" she asks with a snarl. I know she hates them, and I already planned ahead for this.

"They've all been tested recently, and they're clean." I move my mask back in place so I can see her reaction, and the wicked grin lining her face makes my heart skip a beat. She's so fucking excited for this, and I can't lie and say I'm not just as excited.

On a serious note, she turns to the three of them, and says, "I've been told I can't get pregnant…" She chuckles nervously. People never know how to act when hearing that, but of course, our friends answer perfectly.

Nyx replies, "So you're saying we can breed you until you can't walk?"

Sloane smiles at her for making the joke and breaking up the awkwardness. And I wish Nyx could see my thankful smile that's behind my mask.

My friends breeding my wife shouldn't turn me on… but I fear it is.

To distract Sloane even more, my hands start roaming up and down her body, gripping her ass like it's the last time I'll get to feel it. The littlest whimper escapes her. "Are you going to fuck me or just keep touching me all over?"

With that comment, I pick her up without a word and carry her over to our oversized, rustic oak coffee table. A place we've fucked many times. I lay her down, pull my knife back out from its leg holster, place the blade in the middle of her chest, and cut the middle of the bra with a satisfying pop.

I growl at her gasp. "I'll get you a new set." Her perfect tits are free and the bra is still hanging over her arms. I pull the right side of her thong away from her body and slice my knife through those, too. Her bare pussy is peeking at me, with her thong around her left leg still.

I run the tip of my knife along the lower half of her stomach, back and forth, torturously slow. She's up on her elbows, watching my every move with it. "I want to see my toy bleed. Mark you so the others know who you belonged to first." I just sharpened this knife today, so I know it will cut her pretty. She loves to be marked, and I can already tell she's about to beg for it. "That pretty pussy is already weeping for me...or is it for the others?"

Sliding the blade through her skin, I make a small v-cut on the bottom right corner of her stomach. It takes her a moment to register the pain, but when her eyes meet mine, they're practically burning with flames of desire.

They're begging for more, so I give her just that. "Hold still, baby, I don't want to mess my pretty heart up." I curve the knife up and around the first side, and then the other, meeting it in the middle. Once I'm satisfied, my eyes on my beautiful wife's happily beaming face, I pull up the bottom half of my mask and lick my knife clean.

I purr my praise, "You bleed so pretty for me, baby." She has the prettiest of hearts carved into her equally pretty skin.

Rhodes breaks me out of my daze. "Fuck, this is hot."

I look over at him with his huge cock in his hand, pumping it up and down in slow motions. It takes everything in me not to groan.

Fuck, how I've missed men.

Pulling my dick free from my black cargo pants, the relief is instant. I'm pumping myself over her while I instruct her, "Pull those knees up and show me that pretty cunt." I'm quick to get my wife ready for my cock. Even with her already wet enough to make her pussy glisten for me, I spit on it. "Spread it. I need my fuck hole to be wet. Let me see what I'm going to breed."

*Yeah, the breeding kink will never leave me...*even when we know Sloane can't get pregnant.

Me being in full gear and her below me with her shredded lingerie barely hanging onto her body is a dichotomy I didn't know I would love, but we may have to do this more...

Sloane's biting her lip, begging me with her eyes to fuck her. She's still playing into the game of her not wanting this, and it's driving me even madder.

I hear Nyx whisper to Asher beside me, "Isn't her pussy so pretty?"

"Fuck yeah, it is," he groans. I hear him working his cock, too, but I don't even look. There's no way I won't bust immediately if I look at them while fucking my hot as fuck wife.

I question Sloane, "Is my whore ready?"

"Yes, Daddy."

And with a grunt from Rhodes at the *Daddy* nickname, I slam into my wife's greedy, waiting cunt.

I groan as Sloane's head throws back in pure bliss. "Rub your clit for me."

"I can do it." Asher shocks me with his response, but I give him a nod and he's there in a heartbeat beside us. He looks at Sloane and asks her, "Can I?"

"Fuck, yes. Please, Ash."

His breath hitches at the use of the nickname. I watch as he runs both his hands down her stomach, hitting the newly carved up, bleeding heart. He smears some of the blood as he's gripping her hips while humming in appreciation. Sloane hisses out in pain, but Asher keeps going, already knowing she enjoys the pain just as much as the pleasure. One of his big hands pulls up slightly where her labia meets, and his other lands perfectly on her exposed clit.

Thank fuck he knows how to find the little bundle of nerves. Regardless of him being the baby.

"Oh fuck, right there, yes." Asher meets my eyes

while I'm hammering into my wife, and it takes everything in me not to come right there.

I give him the praise I know he'll soak up like a sponge. "That's it, Asher. Make my wife come on my cock." Testing the waters some more, I add, "If you're a good boy, you can clean her up after I'm done filling her." Sloane and Asher both whimper at that, and that's when I really start pounding into her.

Bending my knees, I get the angle I need to hit that spot inside her. I switch to quick, shallow thrusts, rubbing my cock all over that bundle of nerves. Asher's pressure picks up, and he's pulling even harder to keep her clit free.

Nyx is at our other side before I realize it, her lips sucking one of my wife's sandy brown nipples into her mouth while she pinches the other. Sloane's screams are music to my ears. "Fuck! Fuck! Fuck! I'm coming!"

As she's spazzing around my cock, I thrust two, three, four more times, and hold there. Through a clenched jaw, I grit, "I'm coming, baby! Fuck you feel so good for me."

I slowly pull my cock free while Nyx has her mask pulled up still, who is absolutely tonguing my wife's mouth. Asher looks at me innocently. "Can I clean her up now?"

I step away, my cock glistening with my release and Sloane's, as he crawls over in front of her still spread-out pussy, lifting his mask. He runs his hands up the back of her thighs in appreciation and murmurs, "I've only dreamed of this…" Then he's diving in, licking my wife from ass to clit, not missing a drop of my cum.

Once I feel he has Sloane nice and clean, I step up to him, grabbing the top of his mask, including the hair beneath. Leaning down, hovering my lips above his, I whisper, "That's a good boy. Now let me taste." I smash my lips to his. He's stiff for a moment, but quickly lets my tongue in to explore his taste mixed with my wife's and my orgasm.

I look up, and Sloane's eyes are on Asher and me. The pure want in them is breathtaking. "I love you, baby," I confess.

Sloane's quick to respond, "I love you too, Simon."

I hope this whole situation doesn't tear us apart, but at this moment, I don't think anything could, if I'm being honest.

Rhodes pulls me out of my trance with his chuckling. "You got all your fake cocks in there, Nyx?"

Nyx is grabbing her backpack, which I know has all her toys, straps, and fuck knows what else in it. "I don't hate the thought of pegging you fucks. Now, leave us alone or I'll gag all of you with my silicone cocks."

Yep. I'm good on that one.

I'm no stone top, but Nyx pegging me is not on my bucket list…

We guys have found our way to the couch. I'm in the middle of Asher and Rhodes.

Asher leans towards me and whispers, "My cock shouldn't have reacted to that…"

Rhodes leans over the other side of me. "I think you might be a little pansexual, Ash." Rhodes has a shit-eating grin on his face. "Because I am, and my cock did the same thing."

"Mine is twitching with you two leaned over top of me like this. Now fuck off so I can watch my wife."

They don't…

Instead, Rhodes leans in the last little bit to place his lips on Asher's, and I watch in mild shock as Asher opens willingly for Rhodes. I put a hand on the back of their heads, encouraging them. "Mmm, greedy boys."

Oh, this is going to be a fucking wild ride.

8

SLOANE

"How are we doing, pretty girl?" Nyx asks as she towers over me, petting my hair softly. Her words are soft and caring as my chest heaves from the remnants of my last orgasm, but her eyes glint dangerously as she wracks her gaze over my body hungrily. "Think you can handle some more? Because we have a long night ahead of us, ya know."

I groan, both in need and lust. God, I want everything they'll give me.

And then some.

I gasp as her fingers, soft and delicate regardless of her heavy tone, run over the cut Simon left on my lower abdomen. He had never done anything like that before, even when I had asked him to do it when it was just the two of us, and that alone made tonight monumental. The blood coats the lower half of my stomach, and it *hurts*, but it's beautiful all the same.

I would always belong to him now—wedding ring and scars alike—no matter what.

Nyx continues, her eyes bouncing up to look at the guys on the couch. I follow her gaze and refuse to take my eyes off of what I'm witnessing. Rhodes and Asher kiss desperately, Simon's hands on the back of both of their skulls, keeping them together, all while Rhodes slowly begins to pump my husband's cock languidly. "I've never once found men attractive until this moment, but I think I need to bury my strap-on in you and make you cum for me, all while we watch the live porno. Don't you think so?"

I don't take my eyes off the men in front of me. I don't even need to hesitate in response to her question, though. My response is desperately needy. "Please, Mommy."

The resulting and immediate push of a firm, hard length inside of me is the only answer I get back, and my head turns to Nyx at neck-breaking speed as she bottoms out a strap inside me. The moan that tears out of me is guttural.

"Fuck," I moan, nearly shouting, even as my hips lift on their own accord. It forces the boys to turn back towards me for a moment, smirking roughly as they watch my body jostle on the coffee table once more, only to return to their own fun. It's sinful and delicious all at once. "No warning? Fuck me!"

She laughs as she shifts her hips, hitting a spot inside of me that makes my mouth open in a perfect circle. "You were too busy staring at your husband to notice that I had stripped, so I got your attention how I wanted to. This toy lets me fuck the both of us at once, too. Are you okay with that?"

I spread my legs wider, taking her strap-on and nodding my head eagerly. "It's so fucking thick. Oh my God."

Nyx moans on a harder thrust herself. "Yeah it is. Take my strap, beautiful girl. Show these men how much better a woman knows how to fuck."

Rhodes breaks his kiss with Ash, chuckling softly. "Hey now, she hasn't even given us a shot yet."

I don't take my eyes off Nyx. If she weren't wearing the mask that covers her lower face, I'm almost certain I would see her smile ruthlessly as she turns her attention to Rhodes for the slightest moment, only to have the piercing gaze land back on me. "Oh, I'll be giving her two more orgasms before you three even finish once. She hasn't taken a girl's cock in years. Her legs are already trembling for me. I doubt you'll get her to tremble like this."

I moan so loud at her words, just enjoying being the pillow princess for a moment. Enjoying taking her.

Enjoying the sight of tits bouncing in my face as her thrusts pick up speed, fucking us both harder than ever. Taking in the full glory that is this beautiful woman, stretching me more than I have been in a very long time.

Fuck, she really is beautiful.

Her body is absolutely covered in tattoos, with the only piece of blank space being her torso, tits, and chest. It only adds to the dangerously feminine rage she carries everywhere she goes. It's no wonder she never wears makeup, outside of her groomed brows and mascara. She doesn't need to fit within society's norms of a feminine woman whatsoever. The tattoos, long hair—even curled up in a clip now—and aura alone make her more than perfect in my eyes.

Except for…

"Why," I pant out as she continues her movements, forcing my eyes to roll. God, I feel like I could come again already. "Why do you only have one nipple piercing?"

Her actions pause for a moment as she takes in my question, fighting back her own intense pleasure. "It hurt like fuck?" she responds, confused.

I giggle, full of bratty intention all of a sudden, as my own hands go up to twist my pierced nipples. Pain and pleasure mix, and I wouldn't be surprised if I saw my cum as cream on her purple dildo. "Awe, baby Nyx, huh? Topping me when you can't even handle a piercing needle. Looks like you're not as big and bad as you seem, right?"

Within seconds, she's leaning down, forcing the massive length to fully bottom out inside of me. One of her delicate hands wraps around my throat, squeezing the sides aggressively, then I feel her hand crack against my tit. The air is lurched out of my lungs from the mixture of actions, and my eyes bulge. Her hips shift, making the coffee table rock from the force. I can't even moan with her grip on my throat, but *fuck*, it feels so good. "Oh, you wanna be a brat, huh? While I'm making you feel good? Go on, you pretty slut. Try and talk now."

I go to do so, egged on by her goading, but I can't even breathe properly from her choking, let alone speak. She thrusts hard again, and my eyes nearly roll to the back of my skull.

She keeps going, forcing her length inside of me, never letting up on her intense grip. My eyes start to go fuzzy as I stare at her fucking me.

It's the best thing I've ever felt.

"No? Can't speak now, huh? That's right. Just taking your mommy's cock like the good girl you were before you opened your pretty mouth. I should make one of the boys fuck your mouth like this so you remember your place is below us, but I'm too obsessed with you to share."

Oh my *God.*

Finally, she releases my throat, and I gasp harshly as air fills my lungs. The relief is short lived before she's shoving her fingers in my mouth and down as far as she can reach, gagging me herself as she fucks me mercilessly. Drool and spit coats her fingers as she pushes her fingers deeper, easily finding my gag reflex and forcing me to lurch forward.

She lets up slightly, thankfully not pushing too hard to make me sick. Her hand leaves my mouth, smearing my lipstick nearly to my chin, and grabs one of my thighs, forcing my leg up on her shoulder. The new position pushes me to my limit alone, and I nearly vibrate with how close I am. "Oh yeah, sweetheart. Be my filthy slut. Come on my fucking dildo so we can break this little bratty attitude up. Orgasm one out of two. Give it to me."

And then she does exactly what I need to finally make me fall over the edge.

Her dainty fingers on her other hand strum my clit expertly. She moans just as loud as I do when my pussy starts to tighten on her strap-on even more, forcing her to be even rougher with her thrusts, forcing her to fuck herself even harder. With the short end of the toy inside her, I know she has to be close, too.

"Nyx," I moan loudly, locking eyes with her. "Yes, yes, yes!" I shout, right as my orgasm wracks my body. Fireworks may as well have erupted in my veins as my eyes grow hazy and my pussy spasms around her toy wildly. She doesn't let up for a second, though, fucking me harder and faster, milking my orgasm for all it's worth.

"God," she moans, what seems like hours later, and lowers my leg off her shoulder softly. I wince, already feeling soreness, even though we have much more night ahead of us. "I'm never letting you go, pretty girl. That was…"

"Amazing," I finish for her.

She nods, staring at me intently, but it's the sound of a guttural moan from the men beside us that finally breaks the bubble we've found ourselves in. We both turn, and immediately, I can feel myself becoming soaked, even though Nyx hasn't even pulled her toy out yet.

I watch as Rhodes fucks my husband, both of their eyes on me even as they roll back, right as Asher pushes his length into my husband's mouth, shutting him up. The sight alone makes me want to come undone yet again, and I'm immediately reaching for Nyx, needing another orgasm, not wanting to bother the boys.

Simon needs this. He's been needing this for a long time.

It was only fair I let him have his fun, too.

Nyx giggles, pulling out of me, and I groan as I see the mess I left on her toy. She does too, but she just throws it into her backpack without a second glance and reaches for my hand. "Bedroom, baby girl. I need to cum so fucking bad, and I'm hellbent on getting that second orgasm from you."

Achingly, I follow her into mine and Simon's bedroom, without a second glance to the love of my life.

Even if his eyes follow me heavily, all while taking two other men.

9

SIMON

One moment, Rhodes and Asher have the bottom of their masks lifted up as they kiss over my lap while I instinctively push their heads together. The next, Asher's looking up at me, questioning with his eyes. "Can I?"

I'm quick to quip back, "Can you what, Asher? You've gotta use better words than that."

"Can I try to suck your cock, Simon...I haven't do—"

He stops before he can finish, looking shier than I've ever seen this man. All while Rhodes is still on my other side, but his hands are roaming my body and I'm doing everything in my power not to melt into a goddamn puddle on this couch.

I grab Asher's face in my hand, a little more aggressively than I wanted to, and whisper while hovering right above where my hand covers his mouth. "You can suck my cock as long as I get yours in my mouth after." I have a giddy feeling he's packing some fucking heat behind his zipper.

He gives me the slightest nod in agreement. Not even giving him a second, I lift the bottom half of my mask before I smash my lips to his, forcing him to accept my tongue on his. I was always told kissing another man was supposed to feel forbidden while growing up, but I was quick to learn that my body likes what it likes. And that happens to be men *and* women.

Relishing in the little gasp that turns into the sweetest whimper from Asher, I make it my goal to get as many of those noises out of him as I can tonight. I pull back slightly to take his plump bottom lip between my teeth and hold it there just a second longer, which earns me a groan.

I release him, and he slowly opens his eyes, still in his daze. The only thing I see is a pair of blown-out, lust-filled pupils. Almost to the point I can't see his icy blue irises. "Let me see those pretty eyes crying while you choke on my cock, pet."

His eyes almost bug out of his head, but he pulls it together and slides to the floor between my spread-out legs.

Fuck, he belongs there.

On his knees.

Waiting for my commands.

His hands land on my thighs, and I adjust his mask for the majority of it to sit on top of his nose. He's looking a little nervous, but he pulls the waistband of my cargo pants down just enough to spring my cock free again. Remembering how he had just cleaned my cum from my wife's pussy, I question him, "You going to clean my cock up now, pet?"

He grabs me at the base while his eyes are on me. "Suck me like you wish you could suck your own cock." Taking me by surprise, he spits on my dick and his hand, working the saliva up and down my shaft in a few quick strokes.

I watch with rapt attention as he lowers his head onto the tip of me, swirling his tongue around my crown and focusing on sucking the very tip while still pumping up and down. His eyes are burning holes through mine, and I can't look away. Grabbing the sides of his head, I give him the praise I know he needs.

"Good boy," I purr, and that has him melting down on my cock even further. His lips meet his hand, his throat opening with the praise like the little whore I knew he was. He's straddling my calf, and I can feel his hips start to grind down on my leg. "Ride my leg, pet. Don't you dare come in your fucking pants again, though."

I hear a growl come from Rhodes, and a huge, thick

hand wraps around my throat in warning. "Quit teasing him, Simon."

Rhodes turns my head towards him, and I just give him a wicked smile. He knows this is how I am with Asher and that I would never actually want to hurt him, but I also know Asher loves the protective side of Rhodes. And when we both look down at Asher, with my cock stretching his mouth wide, I swear I see his eyes crease a little with a smile.

The grip on the sides of my neck presses in and steals my next breath I so desperately want, causing a little squeak to crawl up my throat.

Rhodes grunts, "I want this pretty ass of yours, Simon."

"Sorry, caveman, you'll have to be nicer than that when asking to take any of my holes." It won't take much more from him, if I'm being honest. The deep-rooted need I've carried around for years in regards to Rhodes is finally getting to come out and explore.

The plug I've had in for hours now is the biggest plug I own, and the way it's been bouncing off my prostate all night has my eyes crossing. Then add Asher deep-throating and gagging on my cock? I could come any second.

I grab the back of his head and practically pull him off my cock, and what does the little shit do?

He whines.

"Simon, I was just getting in the groove! Was it at

least good?!" The sadness lining his features has me ready to feed him my cock again.

"You were perfect, pet. Too perfect. I was about to come down your throat if we didn't stop there." His smile is beaming. "Hop up on the couch and kneel in front of me."

"Fuck yes," Rhodes cheers under his breath, already knowing what my plan is.

I get on my hands and knees in the center of the couch, wagging my ass that is slightly out of my pants. That makes Rhodes move quick. He's behind me, yanking my pants down to my bent knees, and lands a sharp slap to my bare ass.

I wag it one more time, really trying to rile him up. "Mmm, give me another." He does two more quick slaps in the same place, causing me to gasp, but that only spurs him on.

He lands three on the opposite cheek, evening them out, then he's pulling my ass cheeks apart. I know he's examining the plug that's nestled between my globes, and I sure as fuck hope he likes what he sees.

Like he's talking to himself, Rhodes questions, "A plug? You knew to be ready for me, didn't you? Tell me, Simon, how long have you wanted this cock of mine?"

Way too long...but I don't want to sound like a greedy slut, so I give him a grunt instead.

Smack.

I hiss at the sting, but the string of pre-cum that's

leaking from the tip of my cock is giving me away. Receiving pain is a guilty pleasure of mine, even if it's right up there with dishing it out. I haven't been able to be on the receiving end in a long time.

I've missed it.

Fuck, I think I've just missed men.

Don't get me wrong, my wife's body is something I couldn't have conjured up any better myself. She's beyond perfect, ethereal truly…But the strong thigh muscles currently under my hands, beards rubbing together, and the cock that's attached to a man is something I'll always be willing to let my soul drown in.

My head snaps up when Asher's hands pull my mask from my face. He's taken his off, as well, and a warm gooey feeling surrounds me, knowing I'm going to get to see his reactions to the first time he's getting his cock sucked by another man. Asher sounds shy as he asks, "Rhodes, can we see your face, too?"

I should be worried that this will ruin the experience for Sloane, but she's so lost in Nyx at the moment.

Looking over my shoulder, I see Rhodes pull off his blanket-type mask and toss it behind him on the floor. He's grinning at Asher. "You gonna be able to keep from coming in seconds, little one?"

Asher whimpers at Rhodes's teasing, and that spurs me on. I grab Asher's thighs, pulling him closer to me and sliding his pants down as far as I can get them while he's in this kneeling position in front of me.

His cock is bobbing heavy between his thighs, causing a hum to crawl up my throat in appreciation. "Fucckkk. I knew you'd be big, but what the actual fuck is this?"

He's all smiles now. "A magic cross piercing."

"A-fucking-what?"

"One piercing goes from top to bottom through my head." He points out each one to Rhodes and I. And it sure as hell does—the bottom ball to the barbell is at the bottom of his cock. "Then another that goes from side to side. Making a cross. It's only magical because it'll have you seeing stars, the moon, and everything holy."

Rhodes is full-on belly laughing. "I thought I was fucking nuts for having one needle shoved through my cock…but you had two."

"At two separate times, too…the first had to heal up."

I can't hold the laughter back. "Here we thought you were the innocent one of the crew."

My laugh is quickly cut off, gasping, from Rhodes tugging my plug and letting my muscles pull it back into place. He lands a smack on the large plug right after, sending a jolt of pleasure through every fiber of my body as it bounces off my prostate. "Is this pretty hole going to pull me in like this, Simon?"

"Mmm, again, please, Rhodes." I'm clearly not above begging. And he gives me everything I needed and more. He smacks the plug, and I feel his calloused hand reach through my legs and grip my cock in a firm, sure grip.

Without a word, I grip Asher's cock and let my tongue circle over the thick diameter of his tip. The piercings feel so foreign to my tongue, but the guttural moan that leaves Asher is music to my ears. His head is tipped back in pleasure, and I hear the lube bottle crack open from behind me. Rhodes pulls the plug out slowly, and I moan around Asher, causing him to grip my head and slow me down.

I feel Rhodes' thick tip resting against my puckered hole. Then he's leaning over, whispering in my ear. "I know you said you and Sloane are clean, but I can still use a condom if you would be more comfortable."

I pause my sucking to reassure Rhodes with my words, "I need to feel you, Rhodes. I want all of you. Including your cum dripping out of me."

He nips the shell of my ear, growling, "Okay, baby." And I turn to mush for the big man.

His lubed cock runs up and down my ready, begging hole, and I'm a whimpering mess already. I've missed this, but even more so, I don't want to ever go back to just being friends with these humans.

Asher feeds his cock to me this time. I'm too busy holding myself up and trying not to tense with Rhodes about to breach my entrance. I open my throat for him, looking up into his eyes, begging for him to use me like the worthless doll I so need to be at this moment.

I don't want control right now.

I want to give up any and every ounce of control I have over to them.

Give them my all.

Milk them until they're sated and panting. Until their cum is leaking from me like a bred whore.

And that is precisely what they both do.

Asher shoves his cock into the back of my throat, holding my head there, causing me to gag. Right on cue, Rhodes finally pushes in. The shared groans from all of us probably have the girls wondering what's happening over here. They've just moved to the bedroom to do God knows what…but I can only focus on the fullness of being stuffed from both ends.

Rhodes is still once he reaches the hilt. "Tap Asher's thighs if it becomes too much, baby." I give him a quick nod, and Asher gives me a beaming smile. Watching that boyish smile morph into pleasure is a high I'll never come down from.

"This is the hottest thing I've ever seen," Asher pants between thrusts, and I start really working him. I hollow out my cheeks and let Rhodes work me up and down his length from the pure force that is behind him. "Fuck, Simon, you're going to make me come if you don't let up!"

I hum my approval. Needing him to finish for me.

In me.

"Mmm."

Rhodes grips my hips. Low enough where I can barely hear it, he mumbles, "This tight little fuck hole is going to have me coming any second, too."

I let my eyes roll back in pleasure, and that, along with my whimpers from the pounding Rhodes is delivering, seems to push Asher over the edge. "Fuck, Simon, *fucckkk* I'm coming." And I keep him as deep as possible, swallowing every last drop he'll give me.

He pulls my head off his cock with a shocked look on his face. Rhodes pulls me up by my vest, his other hand wrapping around my neck, applying the lightest pressure.

Asher's front is to mine, and he's pressing his lips over my mouth. Being pressed between them while Rhodes is still pistoning into me has me floating to another dimension. Rhodes' hands are all over Asher, too, and Asher's cock is rubbing mine at just the right angle…but it's not enough.

Right as that thought enters my brain, Asher starts to kiss his way down my body. His lips are wrapped around my cock before I have time to process what's happening.

"Whimper for me, baby. You sound so pretty," Rhodes grunts.

And I do just that.

Asher doesn't have a timid bone in his body now with how he's sucking me. I whimper, giving him a courtesy warning. "I'm going to come, pet." I barely get my last word out with Rhodes' grip tightening, stealing my oxygen.

Asher sucks harder in response, and that pushes me over the cliff, free falling into oblivion.

Grunts leave Rhodes as my cock still pulses in Asher's mouth. With a couple more pumps, he's filling my ass up, his cock flinching violently as he groans, "Babbbyyy."

10

SLOANE

I barely make it five steps into the bedroom before I'm shoved against a wall and the feminine curve of a mouth is directly on mine. Nyx's hands hold her mask up just enough for her mouth to cover mine, and it's mere seconds before her tongue invades my mouth, turning me into a melted marshmallow then and there.

Orgasms were nice and all, but somehow, this felt intensely more intimate.

Especially once I hear a moan leave her throat and feel her hands at the back of my neck, forcing us even closer together. I swipe my tongue against hers feverishly, savoring everything the woman in front of me is, aching for her all at once again.

A part of me feels guilty for enjoying this. For missing this, as much as I have. But the other part of me is downright aroused, obsessed, and unbelievably happy.

And it's the boys' moans—Simon's moans—I hear through the thin walls that make my brain whisper, *shut up and enjoy it.*

Finally, Nyx breaks her kiss and lowers her mask back in place, but doesn't remove her hand from the back of my neck. In fact, she squeezes it again. This time feels like more of a reassurance squeeze, than anything else. "Need to use your safe word, my pretty slut? I'd respect it, I'm checking in. I know this is…a lot."

I giggle, both in humor and nervousness. "You're my best friend, Nyx. I wouldn't let this ruin us."

"I might."

"Oh?" I ask, quirking an eyebrow. I don't buy her bullshit for a singular second.

"You're just…" she pauses, moving her other hand to wrap around my waist. "You're perfect. And yes, I think I've wanted you for a long time. But you're still one of my best friends, and now I'm the one who's scared. I've been heartbroken a lot lately, you know."

I somber quickly. "I know. But this, right now, is good. We're good."

She nods. "What about tomorrow?"

"We'll worry about that when it comes."

She nods again. "I'm sorry. I came in here ready to fuck the shit out of you again. Not dump my feelings and insecurity on you. I don't know where this is coming from. It's like, out of nowhere, I'm in my head—it's annoying."

A chuckle escapes me, but an even dirtier idea strikes me at the moment. Something that'll have us both feeling good—both the center of attention—and something that's been on my bucket list for a very long time.

I try to play it coy as I run my hand over her waist, pulling her even closer into me. Our breasts rub against each other, nipples pointed and sensitive from the cool piercings, and I moan low in my throat. "I think you need some attention this time."

She shakes her head. "Nuh-uh. I'm giving you another one. We're not leaving this room until you're shaking for me."

"Oh, I don't think we'll have any problems with that, quite frankly. I think you've learned in a very short time that I can't finish unless my clit is stimulated, too. And there's been something I've wanted to try."

"I'm not following."

The brat in me forces my eyes to roll. I force it out in one breath. "I want to try scissoring."

Immediately, her eyes darken. Her hand is on my throat again, squeezing the sides roughly, forcing a gasp out. My legs nearly fold in on themselves as that damned ache returns, and it's intense. Zero to one thousand, out of nowhere. "God, what a little slut you really are, sweet girl. I was being all vulnerable, worried you'd really want me, and all along, you're in your head, thinking about rubbing your pretty, wet cunt against mine. So filthy. Aren't you?"

She releases her grip slightly—just enough to let me talk. "Yes, Mommy," I whimper. Because fuck, I was vulnerable about everything, too. I had taken today in stride, all the way from Rhodes' cryptic comments this morning to being ambushed by my literal walking fantasy. But this was truly something to talk about tomorrow.

Right now? I wanted to enjoy the woman before me. And we would deal with the consequences later.

"Go lay on the bed," she orders hotly. I feel the sting on my ass as I turn away before I fully recognize it, and it forces a blush to mar my cheeks immediately. Though, I do exactly as she says. I even spread my legs against the cool, green satin sheets teasingly, just to give her the full effect of my neediness.

To show her how bad I need this.

She groans deep in her throat, though within seconds, she's promptly mounted against me, and the moan that leaves my throat as I feel her clit against mine is downright guttural. It's swollen and aching, forcing me to be hypersensitive, but it's somehow so good at the exact same time.

So fucking good.

"That's it, little slut," Nyx groans as she shifts her hips against mine, fully grinding down on my pussy. "Let Mommy ride you. Feel how badly you've made me drip tonight. You like the feeling of my pussy on yours?"

I nod frantically.

I stand corrected. Zero to one *million*, out of nowhere. But I'm sure as hell not complaining.

"I love it, Mommy," I groan, equally rolling my hips up towards her. Her resulting eye roll emboldens me, and it's then I realize I need her to come more than anything else. I need to feel her finish against me. "Mount your little girl. Show me what it's like to have all your attention."

She huffs out a laugh, though it's mixed with a moan. "You've always had my attention, darling. All of us. We just weren't allowed to cross that line."

Our movements continue, nothing but pants and moans filling the air. I can tell Nyx is close, but something is holding her back. Maybe her own head, or maybe she just needs something to really push her over the edge. Then, an idea hits me.

"Nyx, open my nightstand," I pant out.

Her movements pause, her body slick and sweaty from the pent up frustration, though she does what I say and leans over me to open the nightstand. I don't even have to speak for her to put the pieces together, and she moans feverishly as she lunges for the vibrator I have stashed away for Simon and myself. "Fuck yes, little girl. You already know Mommy's body, huh?"

I giggle, but that quickly turns into a moan with her as she switches the wand on. Right at that moment, my men—our men—walk through the bedroom door. My eyes catch on all three of them as they take in our position. They go from spent, used, and exhausted, to antsy within seconds, and I don't even bother to hide my smirk.

Rhodes speaks first, though only grips the door frame instead of entering as he starts pumping his thick length. "Go on then. We'll watch the show."

Nyx giggles herself this time and positions the buzzing vibrator right between us, forcing both of our heads to fall back immediately. She put it on the highest setting, and immediately, fire licks at my veins.

"Fuck!" I shout, already about to come from the sensation. Sweat builds on my own brow now. "Nyx, please. Please, I need you to come with me."

She nods intensely, and I'm cursing her for wearing a mask right now. I want to see the expression she makes when she comes.

You will, my brain responds for me.

This isn't ending tonight.

"C'mon, baby girl. Come for me. Be a filthy slut and fucking come," she says while looking down at me. Then, she turns, and locks eyes with Simon. She speaks to me, all while staring at him. "Come for your Mommy while your husband watches you fucking shatter."

And it's with that, my own eyes locking on Simon's, full of complete and utter heat, that I shatter. For the third time that night. And Nyx falls apart right there with me, body shaking, moaning loud enough that I'm nearly positive we will wake up to an apartment noise complaint tomorrow morning.

11

SIMON

I just watched my wife come undone while rubbing her greedy cunt against my friend's equally greedy cunt…there's no going back to what any of us were before tonight.

And I don't want to.

I want to stay in this happy little fuck bubble, but I don't know how possible that is.

I push those thoughts out of my head, trying to enjoy the last couple of hours I know we have together.

All of us.

The three of us guys are lined up at the end of the bed, cocks in hand, watching the girls come down from what looked like Earth-shattering orgasms. Rhodes dipped into the bathroom to clean up before we all came in here.

A part of me wants to tell Rhodes to get back where he belongs…

In my ass.

But I bite my tongue.

We all placed our masks back on our faces to get back into the roles we were playing, but I fear these aren't roles as much as us just being ourselves.

I want my wife to experience all of them in some way, and that's what has me questioning, "Do I get my wife back yet, Nyx?"

Nyx responds with her head flopping back and forth on the bed while she has Sloane tucked into her side. "You'll have to fight me to get her back, bud." She raises her head, gives me a small sly smile, then winks while flopping her head back down.

The content that is lacing Sloane's body is almost enough for me to climb into bed with them and just let sleep take us.

Almost.

I look at Rhodes, silently communicating with him. He reaches forward, pulling Sloane to the edge of the bed by her ankles. The squeal she lets out is too cute. He growls like the caveman he is. "We're not done with you, pretty thing."

Asher's brows are in his hairline. I'm sure shocked

at Rhodes manhandling her, and it just makes my cock hard again.

Rubbing my fingers over Sloane and spreading her out for us to see, I ask, "You want to fuck my wife's swollen, pretty cunt, Asher?"

She whimpers, looking up at Asher. "Oh, fuck yes. I'll get to put that piercing to work."

Asher strips out of his pants before leaning over her to whisper, "I don't know how long I'm going to last. I've dreamed of this for way too long."

"It's okay, pup, I just need you inside me," she whispers back to him. She lifts the bottom of his mask, freeing his mouth to kiss him.

I look over at Nyx, and the strap on and harness lying beside her, which she must have taken off when they came in earlier. Joking, I tell her, "Rhodes wants you to use that on him." I'm laughing, but I quickly stop when I look at him, and he's smirking like he has a plan.

Rhodes is quick to ask her, "Nyx, can you tolerate men enough to fuck my ass, while I fuck Asher's cum into Sloane?"

I hear Sloane moan again. I thought it was from the visual of what Rhodes was mentioning, but I look back at her and Asher, right as he's sliding three fingers into her.

I have a feeling I'm going to need a full view of what's about to be happening between all of us, but I don't move a muscle.

Nyx is back in her harness already, but I grab Rhodes' face, turning it towards me. "You want me to get you ready, big man?"

"Please. I'm sure that would be Nyx's worst nightmare."

Nyx chuckles while crawling over to Sloane to lay kisses all over her body. "Yeah, it would…"

I grab the lube that's lying on the bed and nod to Rhodes to lay down on the bed. But before I start, I raise the bottom of my mask, do the same with his, and press my lips to his. Not in a rushed or heated kiss, more comforting than anything. I slide my hand to the back of his neck while I lay my body on top of his. Our cocks find one another, and we begin to grind them together, chasing whatever pleasure we can get.

I trail kisses down his strong stomach and kneel at his spread legs on the bed. He pulls them up, and I get a perfect view of his begging hole. Drizzling lube onto my fingers, I circle the puckered entrance as his cock is against his stomach, leaking already.

"Run that cock of yours through her folds, pup. I'm tired of waiting. Our girl's cummed plenty. Let her come on your jeweled cock." Asher groans at my words, but does exactly as I instructed.

His cock sliding through her core is beautiful, and the sounds coming from Sloane are already something I'll be thinking about for years after this.

Asher questions, "You ready, Mommy?" And I'm

happy to my core that I picked the perfect friends who checks in constantly instead of assumes.

"Yes, baby boy, fuck me pleasseee," she groans out her answer as he slides into her.

While twisting one of her nipple rings between her fingers, Nyx asks Sloane, "How are those piercings, Sloane?"

"So, so good, Mommy."

Nyx climbs on top of Sloane's face, pulls the crotch strap over, and instructs Sloane, "Eat Mommy's cunt and make me come." Nyx reaches down her body, finding Sloane's clit, and starts furiously rubbing to get her to come quicker for them.

"I'm not going to last…fuck, this is all too hot." Asher closes his eyes and throws his head back, trying to distract himself.

Rhodes' grunt when I add a second finger has him getting my full attention again. I curl my fingers, pressing into what I know will have him seeing stars. I whisper between us, "This ass is going to be mine here soon."

"It's already yours, Simon." And if that answer doesn't have my heart skipping a beat, I don't know what will.

Sloane's eating Nyx's cunt like her life depends on it to survive, and poor Asher doesn't know where to look. His eyes are bouncing from where my wife's mouth is licking and sucking, to where their bodies are attached, and then to Nyx rubbing her to completion.

And the views must do it for him, or it's the convulsing my wife who's vise gripping his cock as we speak. He rushes out, "I'm going to come. Fuck, Sloane I'm going to—where do you want it?"

She pulls her mouth away from Nyx long enough to tell Asher, "In me, baby boy. Breed me. Make me yours."

Asher presses into the hilt and groans out his orgasm, filling my wife's pussy with his cum. I bite my bottom lip, trying to suppress the groan that wants to crawl out of me at the image of another man's cum dripping out of my wife.

"Does the slut want another one?" I intended that question for Rhodes, but three very different whimpers and groans sound out around the room.

Chuckling, Nyx calls all of them out, "Every one of you is a degrading loving whore—dear God."

"Yes, Daddy, give me another finger."

Nyx grabs Rhodes' face, lowers hers to where her nose almost touches his, and grits out, "I'm your Daddy now." He is frantically nodding his head, and I'm sending my thanks that I get to witness all of this. "Hands and knees, Rhodes. I'll scratch you the rest of the way with my cock you seem to need so badly. And Asher, flip her around so Rhodes can fuck her while he takes Daddy's cock."

Asher whimpers again, and that has Nyx coming after him now. "Mmm, another pansexual slut that wants Daddy's cock, too?"

Asher's brows pull together in a silent question. "I thought I was straight until the couch earlier, and now seeing you like this, and being called Daddy…" he practically moans *Daddy* out, "I think you could be right."

Rhodes says matter-of-factly, "It's not about the parts, it's about the hearts."

And that has Asher beaming with a smile on his face.

Sloane laughs and looks up at Asher. "If that's not an awakening, I don't know what is."

12

SIMON

Rhodes is wiggling his ass at Nyx. She reaches her hand out, and I mindlessly give the lube to her. She's quick to land a smack with her free hand to his ass cheek. He groans, thoroughly enjoying what's happening. He growls and pulls Sloane's body under him in one swift move. "Come here."

I can feel the sexual tension; if I'm honest, they've always had it. I think we all have in some way, shape, or fashion and just never did anything about it...

Until tonight.

Nyx instructs, "Get settled into Sloane and then I'll feed my cock into this tight little hole."

Sloane grips his already leaking cock and starts

rubbing it through her slit. "Fuck you're so wet," Rhodes groans.

"That's not me—that's all Asher that you're about to fuck back into me."

"Fucckk." I'm biting my fist to keep from saying anymore. My cock is painfully hard again just from watching.

In a serious tone, Rhodes asks her, "Are you sure about this, Sloane?"

"Yes, I need you in me. Now." She lines him up at her entrance, and he lowers down slowly.

And right as he's pulling back up, Nyx is at his back hole, ready to go. Lubed toy and all. I see him tense for a second, and then he murmurs, "Do it, Nyx. I need it."

Asher has his cock in his hand, pumping his length, and that has Sloane reaching out to take over for him. I crawl over to the other side of her head, and she's quick to grab my cock and starts the same motion.

Fuck I don't know what to look at. Everyone's features are covered in pleasure, and if I think about it too long, I'll end up busting all over my wife's tits in an embarrassing amount of time.

Quicker than even Asher, and that's bad...

"Fuck me, Nyx, don't hold back. You want our girl to enjoy this, don't you?"

"Hell yeah, I do!" She picks up her speed and starts to angle her cock down to hit his prostate better. I know she's hitting it because he's throwing his head back in pleasure.

"Somebody rub her clit. Make her come, please." The pleading lacing Asher's voice is almost desperate. I know he's right there, and so am I.

I reach one hand down, and so does Asher. He finds her spot first, so I pull my hand back up and practically shove my cock into Asher's mouth, and he doesn't even flinch. Just sucks making a show of hallowing his cheeks for me while holding full eye contact.

This little fuck's head is really going to have me busting.

"Thanks, pup." I give him a soft smack on the cheek, and he moans at that, too.

Dear God, these four are really going to be the death of me.

Leaving Asher's mouth and finding Sloane's hole, which is still occupied with Rhodes' impressive cock. I slide my finger into Sloane's hole beside Rhode's cock, which has his head lifting and finding my eyes. He smirks, leaning down to press his lips to Sloane's.

She's wriggling under Rhodes', I know, on the verge of coming any second. I press upward slightly on Rhodes' cock, sending him to that perfect spot inside her.

He pulls away, breathless. "Fuck. Fuck. Fuck, she's squeezing me so tight. I'm gonn—"

Right in his ear, I demand him, "Breed her. Breed

my fucking *wife*." Sloane whimpers from my disgusting words, but I know she's eating this up and *will* be begging for more.

And with a roar, he does just that, pumping that perfect cunt so full of him. I want to watch it drip from her. With that thought and the pressure she's gripping me, I come all over her perfect tits, and Asher is panting, following the lead right behind me.

Asher whispers, "We've made a mess…"

"Be a good boy, and clean Mommy up."

I SCOOP THE TIRED BODY OF MY BEAUTIFUL WIFE UP IN my arms and make my way to our ensuite bathroom. They know they can use the hall bathroom if they want to shower, and frankly, at this moment, I couldn't care less.

I need this time with her.

To make sure she's still feeling okay after everything we just did.

After crossing the line with not just one of our best friends, but three of them.

I sit her down on the sink, whispering to her, "Sit right here for a second; let me get the water to the satanic temperature you love."

She gives me a giggle, and that is exactly what my soul needs in this moment. I reach into our stand-up shower, turn the water on, check it, and head back to scoop her back up. This time, I make her straddle my waist, and not even seconds later, I can feel the mixture of cum running down my length. I'm gritting my teeth, trying not to get hard again. She needs her care and rest before I can have her body again.

I shift us to where the water is washing over both of our bodies, and she lets out a little sigh of contentment. I question her, "How are you feeling, baby?"

She leans her head back into the water and groans out her response, "So, so, good."

"Are you okay to stand?"

She gives me one of her signature bratty-eye roles. "Yes, Simon. I'm not some fragile, frail thing."

I sit her down, and she sways a little. My eyebrows pull up in a questioning gesture, but she just gives me a playful smack on my chest. I grab her shampoo off the shelf and start to massage it into her scalp. The hope that my dick wasn't going to get hard is long gone.

"Ignore it. I'm sorry," I whisper as she looks down at my cock that apparently has a mind of its own, and clearly isn't worn out from all the activities we've participated in.

She runs a gentle fist over my length, almost in appreciation. "I love when you get hard while you're taking care of me. It shows me that you actually care to do this."

"I know, but it's stabbing you in the stomach." I tilt her head back, rinsing the first shampoo out and grabbing some more. That was the first thing she was sure to teach me when this started becoming our thing after the wild scenes we would have. Once that's fully rinsed, I condition her ends and rinse it, as well.

I run my soapy hands all over her body, but stop at the bloodied heart and smile, knowing it's going to mark her perfect stomach so pretty.

She looks up at me with those pleading eyes. "I don't want this to change anything between us or any of them."

I assure her, "It won't, baby. We were just playing the game."

EPILOGUE
SLOANE

"Nyx, I'm freaking the fuck out. Tell me this isn't happening right now," I groan, sitting on the edge of my couch with my hands rubbing nervously over my face. I feel like there are popping candies in my veins with the amount of nerves coursing through me, and it's unbelievably terrifying.

"Hey, hey, hey. Baby girl, it's okay. This is okay. You have PCOS, ya know. Didn't your doctor say you couldn't get pregnant again? Or, well, it was super unlikely, right? Maybe it's just the irregular cycle symptoms again."

I nod my head, trying to settle my breathing, even though my hands still continue to tremble slightly with the panic coursing through me. "Yeah, she did. Especially after Simon and I miscarried a couple years ago. The two combinations, plus the testosterone blocker, make it super difficult. Simon and I haven't used protection in years, and we haven't had any scares. But this just…I dunno, Nyx. Something feels different." I don't say it, but it feels way too similar to the early symptoms of my last pregnancy…

Nyx kneels in front of me, forcing my eyes onto hers. Our gazes clash—one anxious, on the verge of an utmost panic attack, and the other patient and caring. And even in the moment of panic, pain, worry, and fear…it's this moment alone that I know I am utterly in love with the woman before me.

Definitely not the time to voice it, though.

It's been two months since that night, and somehow, absolutely nothing changed in any negative fashion with our dynamic at all. Instead, it only grew stronger, and we all have become a unit.

Sure, the sex is still as depraved, needy, and raunchy as it was the very first time. It has still yet to slow down, and I'm honestly worried my clit is going to fall off any day now with how much attention I have been receiving over the last two months.

But at the exact same time, I have never been happier.

Simon and I had never been happier.

This is what we needed. Simon and I had worried that things would change, and that maybe this well and truly would have been a one-night game to everyone, and yet…I don't think anyone in our group was okay with that. So we decided that it would always be us. All five of us, forever.

Exclusive in a way that didn't make sense to anyone else, but it absolutely makes sense to us.

But a fucking *baby?* A pregnancy? That has to be a way to ruin a polyamorous, happy bubble. Especially with my luck on how fucking-*fantastic* pregnancies seemed to go with my body.

The sickening, aching thoughts pound through my skull in a rushing, emotional tandem.

They're gonna leave.

Simon and I will be alone.

Again.

To fight though this emotionally taxing situation, and hopefully make it out to see the other side again.

We were happy alone before, sure. But could we survive it again, after living in a dream for so long?

Nyx's hands cover my own, forcing the trembling sensation to still as she shifts even closer to me on the floor. "Come back down to Earth, pretty girl. I need you to talk it out for me. I can see you spiraling without even being in your brain, and we both know that's not healthy. What's going through your head right now?"

"You're all going to leave me and Simon if that test

is positive, and then I'm probably going to lose the baby again, and everything in my life is going to fall apart right in front of me." The words burst out of me in a rushing, panicked sentence, and I'm surprised Nyx could even understand it.

She sighs. "Oh, baby. Why do you think we would leave over that? This could be an amazing thing. We could be a *family*, you know?"

A hysterical laugh bursts out of me as tears well in my eyes. "Oh yeah. You, who doesn't like men, are forced with three of them forever. Rhodes, who doesn't believe in love anymore. Asher, who is young and could absolutely bail and start over. Simon, who would be upset we're going through this again. It's not really looking all that peachy over here, Nyx."

She sighs again, leaning up and gently tucking my hair behind my ears before using her thumbs to wipe away the tears starting to fall down my face. Her silver and black rings rub against my face at the motion, bringing a grounding, yet cooling effect. I take a deep breath at the sensation. "First of all, the boys are growing on me. I may identify as a lesbian, but my heart has room to change, okay? Just because I don't want their parts on me doesn't mean I haven't or won't let them into my hearts. Labels suck, and we're doing our best to figure it out. Okay?"

I sniffle and wipe my nose as I keep my gaze locked on hers. "Okay."

"Secondly, we may not have had this talk yet, but all four of us—me, Rhodes, Asher, and absolutely Simon—are madly in love with you. We are obsessed with you. And a baby—a literal, mini *you*—is not going to change that. Okay?"

My heart nearly splits in half at the affirmation and the tears are really falling now. "Okay."

She nods her head in a soothing manner before reaching for her phone, glancing down, and throwing it back on the soft rug below us. "Good girl. Everything is okay. We don't even know if you're pregnant yet, anyway. There's still two minutes left on the timer."

"Yeah," I sniffle, "maybe it's all in my head. I don't know. I've just never gone a full sixty days without my cycle."

"I know. I get that. Have there been any other symptoms?"

"Ermmm…headaches, definitely tender boobs, I've been so fucking tired the past three weeks, and certain smells make me need to run away—chicken, specifically." I make a show of gagging, but it's sadly not a show. The gagging doesn't stop. "But I just assumed you people were wearing me out, more than anything."

She laughs lightly at that, though keeps staring at me, and I stare right back at her. She leans in slowly, brushing her lips against mine in a soft, comforting kiss, before leaning back and continuing to stroke my cheeks with her thumbs. "That could be true, too, honestly. But it's a good thing we're having you take the test to make sure. Yeah?"

I nod. "Better safe than sorry."

She nods back, right as the timer on her phone goes off. A mixture of emotions stir in my stomach from the sound simultaneously.

Queasiness, from the nerves.

Terror, from the potential news about to cover all of us.

And…somehow…even more terror, because amidst all the fear…there are butterflies about the potential of a future baby, when I had lost all hope of that with my little angel.

"Do you want me to look first? Or do you want to?"

I shake my head and force myself to stand. "I'm a big girl. I got this."

And I do.

It takes less than seven strides to reach the hallway bathroom—the bathroom where literally all of this started with Rhodes' cryptic reassurances and hints—before I flip over the test and stare at the result in front of me.

The result that only makes the butterflies grow and the sobs wrack my body, for the absolute unknown that I'm about to face.

Hours later, I find myself curled in a ball with Nyx on the couch, watching yet another comfort movie. After I had my panic attack, where she somehow talked me through it once again, we had collapsed in a heap of exhaustion, and neither of us has moved.

A part of me felt bad. She probably has to pee. But I didn't want to lose her warmth just yet.

My phone buzzes against my jean pocket, and I groan as I grab it. I don't bother shielding away from Nyx, knowing there's nothing that could be hidden from either of us at this point…and knowing it's our boys, from the way her phone simultaneously went off with mine.

PLAY THE GAME GC
SIMON

> On the way up, pretty ladies. How's my wife feeling?

RHODES

> You just love rubbing 'my wife' in our faces, don't you, asshole?

ASHER

> You guys know we're all standing next to each other in the elevator, right?

SIMON

Yes, and yes. Fuck off, the both of you. How's my wife?

SLOANE

I'm okay. Ready for cuddles from all four of you right about now, though.

We need to talk, too. Please.

Nyx says that sounded ominous. But like, we need to talk.

RHODES

Definitely ominous, baby girl.

I sigh as I toss my phone back down and snuggle into Nyx's chest. She wraps an arm around me, kissing the crown of my forehead, before whispering, "We're all gonna be okay. Everything is okay."

I only nod my head.

Mere minutes later, the front door swings open, and all three of our boys stroll in. My eyes immediately catch on Rhodes, who looks more anxious than anyone as his nervous eyes connect with mine, and my heart immediately aches for him.

For a man who always said he didn't believe in love after his bitch of an ex-wife…he looks like otherwise right before me. And even I don't know how to fully process that.

Especially not when it's right at me.

Simon reaches me and leans down, kissing me

softly. "How we feeling, pretty girl? You don't feel hot. That's a good sign."

I smile at him, regardless of the nerves in my stomach. The man makes it hard not to. "I'm okay. Just really tired."

Nyx interrupts us. "Where's my kiss, bro?"

Simon arches a brow in her direction. "Do you really want my mouth on you?"

She crosses her arms, faux annoyance on her face even as I read the humor in her eyes well. "No. But that doesn't mean you couldn't at least attempt it. I feel like chopped liver over here."

Simon shrugs and leans over, but doesn't make it anywhere near her face before Nyx's nails are pinching and snapping at his ear, forcing a pained shriek to fall from his mouth. Simultaneously, everyone bursts into a fit of giggles, and warmth truly begins to seep back into my bones at the comfort we all have with each other.

Simon shakes his head, mutters, "Bitch," and steps away before sitting in his favorite gaming recliner. Rhodes leans against the side of the chair, arms crossed and muscles bulging, while Asher slings himself on the floor, groaning softly as his body melts into the black rug.

Oh, to be so young again that you choose the *floor* over the other couch.

All eyes fall on me as Rhodes asks gruffly, "You said we needed to talk?"

I swallow. Immediately, my throat feels dry and panic wants to overtake me again.

Simon speaks next, and a nervous edge coats his voice. "Is this about us? All five of us? Because…if it is, I think we should talk alone, right? Or am I wrong? I don't know how this works, either."

My brows scrunch up. "What? No. Of course not. I'm happy with us. Nothing is wrong there."

Rhodes, Asher, and Simon visibility relax more at the confirmation, and my heart tugs at the realization.

They all assumed I was about to break us up.

They were all terrified over it, too.

Fuck, I really need to work on my communication.

Rhodes speaks again, toeing the carpet with his boot. "So, what's going on in that he—"

"I'm pregnant!" I blurt out.

Nyx is the only one who doesn't react, of course, and instead, rubs my arm comfortingly. She's probably worried I'm on the verge of another panic attack. Truthfully, I don't know if I am or not.

"Come again?" Simon asks, as Rhodes stands up straight and Asher sits up. In seconds, Simon has left his chair and is squatting right in front of me, with nothing but love in his gaze.

It soothes me more than anything.

I lock eyes with him, before turning to Rhodes and Asher, who have somehow ended up standing right next to each other in the time Simon moved in front of me. Both look nearly frozen in place, and although the sight makes me worry, it's Simon's touch on my small stomach that forces me to keep speaking. "I took a test this morning. Multiple tests after, too. I'm pregnant."

Simon's face lights up like a Christmas tree, and tears immediately spring to my eyes.

But it's both Asher and Rhodes moving, Asher squatting next to Simon, and Rhodes sitting right beside me, that force the tears to fall as a shuddering breath escapes me.

They're not running.

Asher speaks for the first time. "And…ya know, it's ours?"

My eyes roll. "Obviously. I just…I don't know exactly who's, I guess."

Rhodes reaches down, covering Simon's hand with his own, and Asher does the same. "Baby, that doesn't matter. We're a unit, yeah? That baby is ours no matter what."

I blush, and stutter through my next set of words. "I mean. It doesn't have to be. You guys have an out if you want it. It's not like it can be Nyx's baby. And if you all don't want to be dads…you can have the out, right? Even if it hurts me."

Simon groans. "I'm gonna punish you for that later. Why would you think any of us would want out of this baby? We can be a true family now. Do you know how much this little one will be loved? My God, it'll be the most spoiled child ever."

I smile, but freeze at the same time. "We lost the last one. What happens if w—"

Rhodes interrupts me this time, pressing his hand even firmer on my tummy, forcing butterflies to flutter furiously. "We will deal with any negatives if the negatives come. But this, Sloane? This isn't a negative, baby. Not to us."

I can't help the tears falling now.

Two panic attacks, pretty much, for nothing.

Story of my fucking life.

"So, you're all in? You wanna have a baby? You wanna start a family?"

"It may not be mine by genetics, obviously, but that child is definitely mine, too," Nyx says, smiling next to me.

"Of course I'm in, silly," Simon says, kissing me softly again. "You're the love of my life. I'm never going anywhere. Ever."

Rhodes speaks next. "I've wanted this for years. I've wanted true love and a family for years. I have one now. Don't give me an out, because I'm not gonna fucking take it. Even if I'm old and brittle."

Simon shoves at him. "We're the same age, asshole. Correct yourself."

All eyes turn to Asher, who's only staring at my stomach with a starstruck gaze. Simon nudges him slightly, and he turns to me, smiling ear to ear. "What? I already called her Mommy before. I just get to call her that every day now, fuckers."

And in that moment, with everyone touching me and loving me more than I've ever been loved in my entire life...I have the feeling that everything will truly be okay.

Because the game is now the long haul.

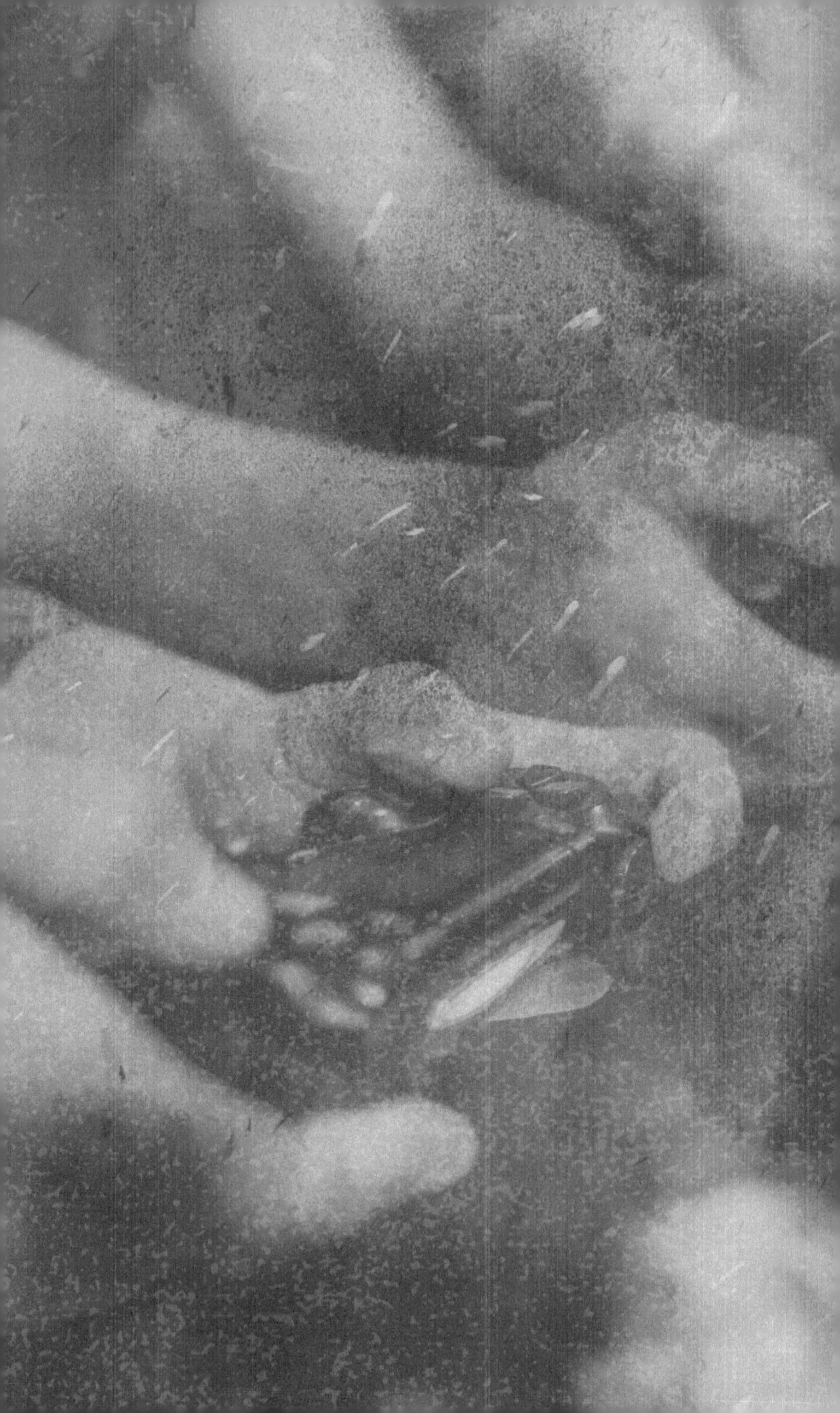

ACKNOWLEDGMENTS

FROM C. S. SILVERNE

Man, I truly suck at writing these sometimes, but I'm absolutely honored to be able to do so—so, here we go :)

To Tilly, first and foremost, because… holy shit, we really wrote a story together? When you first published your debut, I was quite literally just a fan/reader, and now we're becoming best friends and co-authors. That's insane. But I could not be happier and prouder for us both. <3 You're stuck with me forever now bby.

To English Proper Editing Services, who is truly my go-to girl, and handles all of my chaos in absolute stride. Her comments/reactions are legendary, her vibe is authentic, and her work is impecable. Cheers to yet another filthy story with even more to come.

To Anna, who is absolutely stuck with me now too. I'm so happy to be able to call you a friend now.

To Bria, who quite literally helped my social media game to the point that this could actually be a thing. You rock more than you know, and I'm so grateful for you.

To my ride or dies—Katie, Eli & Sierra—who support me through the thick and thin. I love you weirdos.

To the masked community that inspired this entire thing (excluding the ones who have hurt the bookish community and/or authors, because… c'mon now. Stop it). Stay kinky, stay weird, and stay hot. I'll continue drooling from the sidelines forever more.

To the readers who take our filth with eager hands. I adore you.

And lastly, to T, who didn't even blink when I told him that I wanted to write a *Call of Duty* orgy novella. If anything, you promised to dress up for me next, which… oof—yes please? But really—you're my best friend, and I couldn't do any of this without your love and support. My yellow heart, always. Thank you.

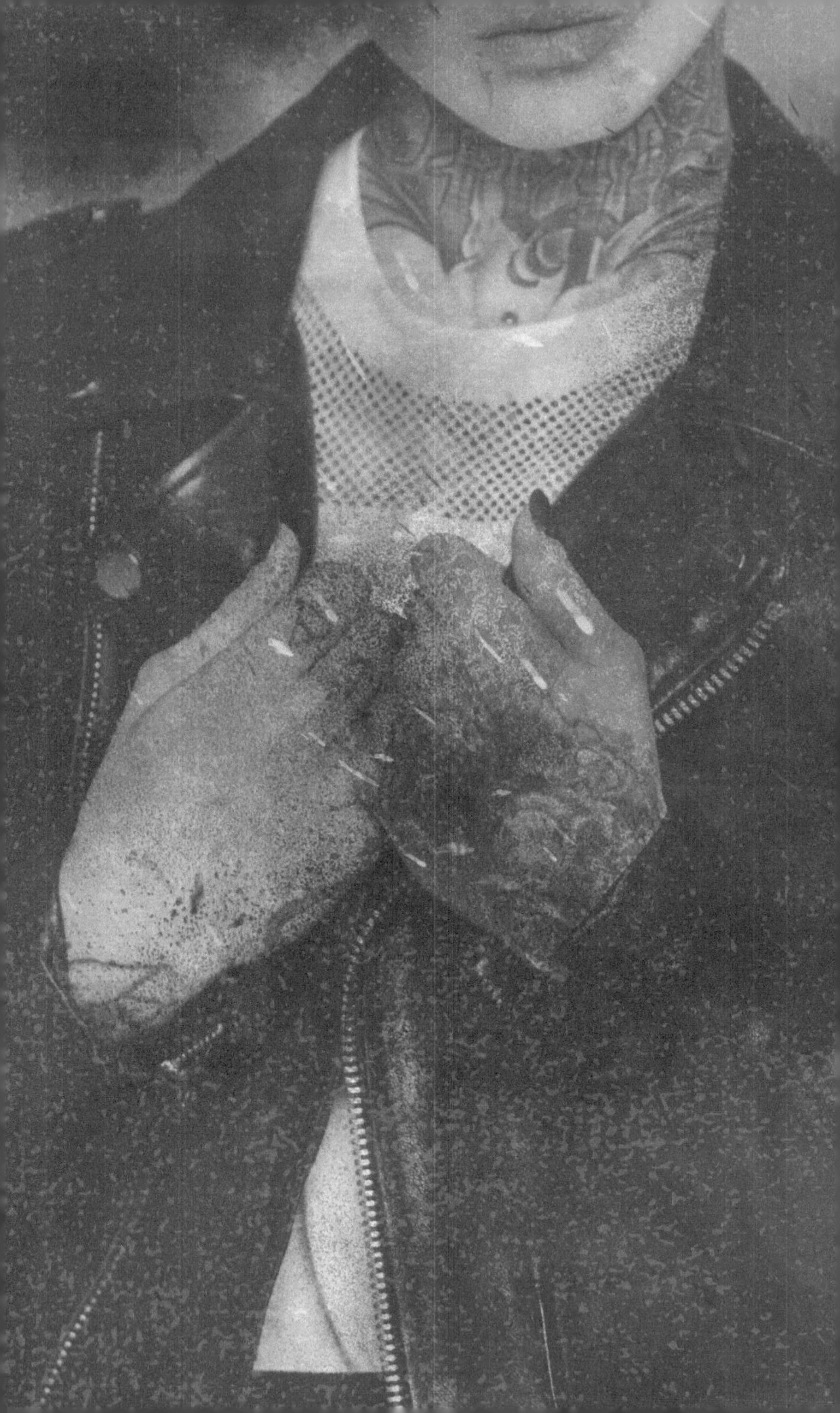

ACKNOWLEDGMENTS

FROM TILLY RIDGE

This whole book came from C.S. messaging me a COD thrist trap and following it up with, "We're never allowed to go to a COD party."

And I followed that up with "WAIT ARE THOSE A THING?!"

Bam! Here we are.

This book was also being refered to as "COD orgy Party" for way too lol.

This was nothing less than a fever dream… really a

fever dream of both of us getting sick twice during the quick writing process. It was so worth it, though!

C.S., you were a dream to write with, and I'm so glad you said yes to this wild idea (which seems to be the norm of our friendship at this point). Love you so so much, and our little book baby we have now!

Anna. Our little bb bear. The one I'm lucky enough to call my PA. Thank you for doing so much for this book and its release. You're amazing, and we love you so, so much!

Paige, Corrina, and Delaney, thank you for reading this early as Alpha readers! It means the world to us to receive your feedback!

To our ARC readers, thank you all for taking the time to read this early and taking the time to review our little ol' book. It truly means the world to us indie authors!

And you all. The readers, thank you as always! Neither of us would be where we are without you!

WANT MORE

FROM C. S. SILVERNE?

While many ideas are constantly brewing, feel free to check out the following titles for more in the C. S. Silverne world <3

Prideful Ache: An Age Gap MC Erotic Novella

featuring a masked man, brat/brat taming kinks, and more.

Longing for More: A Forbidden Military MFM Novella

featuring a Marine Corp men, breeding kinks, and more.

Contrition: A Second Chance MFM Rockstar Romance

featuring a runaway husband, brothers who share, groveling, and… cucking.

WANT MORE

FROM TILLY RIDGE?

Masked & Mine: An MMF Dark Romance

Read here!

Want Mar's story and her two masked men she has on their knees?

@devils_sovereign : Marfa, but call me Mar.

I'm just your favorite devilish cam girl looking to showcase my assets to my loyal demons. I was encouraged to take on this new persona as a cam girl by one of my clients at my former place of employment, "Sins: In Sin City," and here I am thriving. Sins is the biggest and most reputable sex club in Vegas, and well, I just got fired yesterday. Not for anything I did, but because my father is the leader of the Russian Mafia. Now I'm stuck, needing to put my all into this cam girl gig if I want to survive living in Vegas.

@Untrained__Ghostt : Mack

To many, I'm known as a tattoo shop owner and artist by day, and in the words of my subs, a "drool-worthy" cam guy by night with the persona of Ghost from Call of Duty. Together with my partner, Percy, whom I met through TikTok, we have been camming for the best subscribers ever. Tomorrow we're meeting with the first person we are going to collaborate with. The first girl I've been with in years—let's see how this goes…

@Königoftheunderworld : Percy

I'm a marketing firm manager and a little bit of a control freak, but underneath the boring, my real self comes alive when I cosplay as König when camming with my partner, Mack. I've never been happier, and everything has been perfect, but the pessimist in me feels it's a little too perfect. I've been feeling a little apprehensive about sharing Mack, but I know it's been something we've both been wanting to dip our toes into. It doesn't, however, make me any less anxious about losing control.

<u>Playing for the Dark & Taking Over the Dark</u>: A Completed Duet: A Why Choose Mafia Sports Romance

Las Vegas.

The City of Sin.

What happens here, stays here.

There's only one man in charge: Marcello Barone, leader of the Italian mafia. He's ruthless and unhinged. His only weakness? Ellie Dixon.

For the last year she's maintained her calloused attitude toward men, but at the persistent pursuit from two players of the Vegas Rebels, she finds herself welcoming a little fun.

Nash Hayden, quarterback and number one draft pick, isn't used to the fast life. As he begins his new life, he finds his devotion to his father falters as his spirituality evolves, contradicting everything he thought he knew from his Texas upbringing.

Zamir Prifti, a wide receiver with Albanian mafia ties, does everything he can to hide the darkness woven into his soul. What he doesn't know is how far his family is willing to go to get him back.

Will Marcelo's unwillingness to share sever the connection they've formed?

Or will they learn to play together?

Las Vegas

The City of Sin

What happens here, isn't what it seems.

Marcello has finally decided to share his life, his secrets, and his trust, with people he never saw coming. However, that trust is put to the test when Ellie and Nash disappear, and it all points to Zamir.

Will Marcello and Zamir be able to put everything else aside in order to save Ellie and Nash?

Or in the city of lights, will the darkness finally take over?

**A dark why choose romance. This book is only meant for an 18+ audience. Please read the content and trigger warnings on my website.

All future projects will be found here and uploaded as I finish the chapters. Character art prints, early access to all news, getting to pick character names, signed copies sent on release months, and so much more!

Click here for my Patreon.

The Tales of the Scorned Anthology: A Femme Rage Charity Anthology: Paranormal and Dark Romance Stories

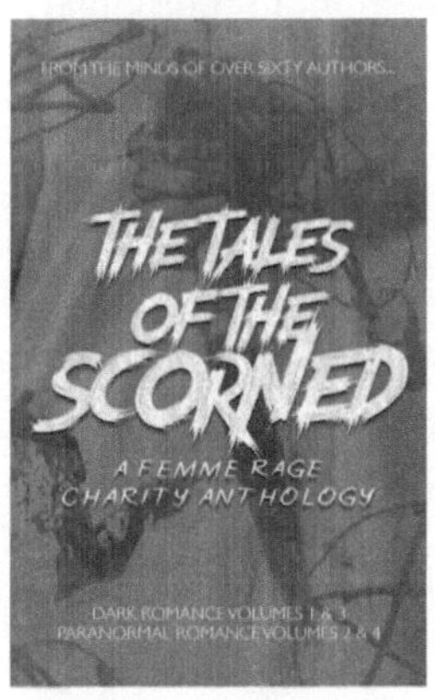

If you loved the femme rage from Ellie in this duet (mainly in book two), I think you'll love The Tales of the Scorned Anthology!

The Tales of The Scorned: All Dark and Paranormal Stories is included in this E-book

Welcome to The Tales of The Scorned, where offenders may, or may not, make it out alive.

From the minds of over sixty authors, we bring you all new stories. Each story will be filled with pure femme rage.

All proceeds from both paperbacks and E-book will be donated to three organizations that fund, provide, and benefit reproductive rights within the United States.

The Tales of The Scorned Anthology volumes will only be available for a limited time! Grab your copy today!

No participating authors, organizers, or service providers are affiliated or endorsed by any of the chosen organizations. We are a community of individuals bound together by a single wish, to protect the right to reproductive healthcare in all forms.

Triple Threat: A Reverse Harem Halloween

Short Story

Triple Threat is my newsletter freebie! It's skull face painted triplets with one lucky gal, making all her fantasies come to life!

Strong Side: An MM College Sand Volleyball Romance

Read here!

Clayton Aldrich is everything I'm not, and everything I

despise. He's rich, never had to work for anything a day in his perfect life, is the pretty boy on campus, and is always doing everything he can to get under my skin. But when we're forced to become partners, I have no choice but to set my predisposed feelings for him aside. However, as the season progresses, two things become abundantly clear. There's more to Clay than meets the eye, and my feelings for him don't appear to be so black and white.

My entire life has been mapped out for me since the day I was born. Major in business, dedicate every moment of spare time to volleyball, win the Olympics, and when the time comes, take over my father's company. And the only part of that plan that didn't make my skin crawl was playing the sport I loved. Rockwell Campos, the infuriatingly cynical man I feel an inexplicable draw toward whenever he's near, thinks he has me all figured out. But, when we unexpectedly become partners our senior year, Rocky shows me there's more to life than sacrificing who you are and who you want to be in order to be part of a family. Sometimes the families we find are stronger than the ones born in blood.

The two of us may share the same goal, but the question remains… is our strong side, strong enough?

ABOUT
C. S. SILVERNE

C. S. Silverne is a twenty-something year old author who spends a lot of her time hiding behind a computer as the true introvert she is—between writing words, designing pretty pictures, reading her kindle, or blaring the latest rock music release—it's guaranteed she's trying to ignore the world in some emo fashion.

Even in her dark/forbidden and occasionally taboo writing styles... she takes light of her pseudonym, always finding love in the silver linings of the world. Because, as we all know, sometimes—love chooses us in the strangest, cruelest of ways, and the stories of the forbidden deserved to be told.

https://www.cssilverneauthor.com/

ABOUT
TILLY RIDGE

Tilly Ridge is a romance author who resides in the middle of nowhere, Kentucky, with her husband, two kiddos, and two dogs. She loves to dabble in a variety of romance topics, themes, and subgenres, but you'll typically find her writing in the dark and polyamory sections of the shelves. Tilly can be easily identified by the pink slush clutched in one hand while her laptop is in the other, ready to write whenever the mood—or the character—strikes! In her free time, she enjoys playing sand volleyball in her local rec league. But what she finds most exciting is her podcast, Releasing Romance, where she shares her knowledge and experience about indie publishing, often bringing on guests to discuss the ins and outs of indie publishing from different professional points of view! This podcast is a passion project of Tilly's as she finds true joy in helping and educating others in a way that is easy to understand.

Join Tilly's readers group for exclusive BTS, art drops, first looks at pretty much anything, and even chapter-by-chapter releases of her ongoing projects at: Tilly's Thots

The newsletter is where the fun is, and maybe even a free ebook will hit your inbox after—along with a first look at the big news.

Find everything you'll need to stay connected at https://www.tillyridgeauthor.com/links